BIGGLES FLIES SOUTH

BIGGLES
FLIES SOUTH

★

CAPT. W. E. JOHNS

Brockhampton Press

First printed 1938
Seventh impression 1951
This edition first published in 1963
by Brockhampton Press Ltd
Market Place, Leicester
Printed in Great Britain
by Richard Clay and Company Ltd
Bungay, Suffolk 63.8

CONTENTS

AUTHOR'S NOTE

In using a background of historical fact for fiction an author invariably lays himself open to criticism, and the reason is easy to find. Over a period of time, supposition can come to be accepted as truth, even by historians, regardless of the fact that there is no evidence to support the assertions. The result of this is that historians themselves are often at loggerheads, each writer endeavouring to prove that the others are wrong, pointing out that there is no evidence to support their statements, glossing over the fact that there is no evidence to support his own, either. When dealing with episodes which are unsupported by evidence, the imagination is apt to run riot.

Of the assumed facts round which the present book is written we know very little. We know that Jupiter Ammon existed, and we know precisely where the famous Oracle was situated, because the ruins are there to prove it. But when we have said that, we have said all. It is fairly certain that Cambyses' army was lost in the desert. But where? From its last camp the ill-fated army might have ended up anywhere within a radius of a thousand miles. If, as we are told, it started off with the avowed intention of sacking Jupiter Ammon, we can visualize its probable line of march – but that is not to say that it adhered to it. Of the alleged Lost Oasis we know nothing. There may not be one. It is therefore manifestly impossible for anyone to say that a remnant of the army did, or did not, reach this legendary refuge. The oasis, if it exists, might be anywhere within an area of more than 50,000 square miles.

Let us, then, be clear on this point. There is not a scrap of evidence to prove that the lost army ever reached the Lost Oasis; conversely, there is no evidence to show that it did not. Yet the two, over a period of years, have become closely associated. In the following pages I have, quite frankly (and pardonably, I think), assumed the lost army and the Lost Oasis to be where they best suited my purpose. If this seems improbable, or at variance with common belief, it should be remembered that from the historical viewpoint we are dealing not so much with facts as with theories – and theories can be proved, or disproved, with equal facility.

W. E. J.

PROLOGUE

1. *'The King has Spoken'*

MAZEUS, son of Hystomannus, leaned against the warm trunk of a royal palm and regarded with brooding eyes the endless sands that rolled away from his feet to the far horizon. What lay beyond that mysterious belt of purple-blue that veiled the distance, he wondered. What strange beasts dwelt there? Perhaps, those legendary monsters of which he had heard so much, the unicorn and camelopard. He thrilled at the thought of beholding them in the flesh, for Mazeus was young, barely sixteen years of age, and this was his first campaign with the mighty Persian host in which his father was a Captain of the Royal Guard, now encamped on the Oasis of Khargah, in Upper Egypt, the sinister land of that potent godhead, Ra.

The year was 525 BC, nearly five centuries before the Roman Caesar landed on the shores of barbaric Britain. Cambyses, conquering son of Cyrus the Great, founder of the Persian Empire, was on the march, adding more and more territory to his wide-spread kingdom. Egypt had fallen under the pikes and scimitars of his armoured warriors, and he had celebrated the event by destroying the sacred Apis and plundering the temples of the high priests. And now he paused at the oasis to refresh his troops, before moving on to conquer new worlds.

9

But strange rumours were current in the camp. With bated breath the superstitious soldiers told of strange signs and stranger portents, of crafty sorcerers caught in the act of casting spells, and fanatic necromancers who died with a curious light of triumph in their eyes; of pillars of smoke that rose from the desert by day and mystic fires that blazed in the heavens by night. Yet, when the furious Persian scouts had galloped out, they found – nothing. Some spoke of evil shapes seen slinking in the dunes, of double-headed cats, men with heads like dogs, and other horrors never seen before; yet not one could they slay. One archer vowed that he had seen his arrow pass through the body of a twin-faced hawk, yet it did not fall, and a slinger claimed that his stone had bounded from a hydra-headed snake which vanished on the open sand where there was not a hole, or bush, or any other hiding-place. It was all very mysterious.

Mazeus turned from his musings and saw his father striding through the serried ranks of resting men; his face was grave, and Mazeus felt a thrill of apprehension, for his father had been in council with the king.

'What news, O Father?' he asked, as the bearded captain reached their silken tent.

Within the restful shade Hystomannus placed his hands upon the shoulders of his son, a gesture of affection seldom shown. 'You were over young for this campaign,' he said thoughtfully. 'Would that I had left you with your mother in Persepolis.'

'Over young, sir?' cried Mazeus in surprise. 'Why, all the sons I know, many much younger than I, have been to war.' Which was true, for in those distant days boys were trained in the use of arms as soon as they could bear them.

'That may be so,' answered his father moodily, mopping the perspiration from his face with a towel. 'But this is different.'

'How so, my Father? Have I not acquitted myself in battle?'

'Yes – yes. But now – I do not know. These pagan gods – within my heart there is a fear that neither common sense nor reason can dispel.'

'You mean – the king has spoken?'

'Yes. And he acts against the advice of all of us. This passion for strife is going to his head, I fear, until he knows not where to stop.'

'You mean – he will go on?'

'When the sun goes down we march – forward.'

Mazeus's dark eyes opened wide. 'Forward!'

Hystomannus pointed a finger at the shimmering, sun-scorched sand. 'There lies our path,' he said grimly.

'For what purpose, Father? Have we not enough plunder already?'

'More than enough; but Cambyses swears to sack the Temple and destroy the outlandish gods at Ammon. Rumours have reached him of this place, which is near a citadel called Siwah, the home of all the witchcraft in this thrice-accursed land, where none can quench his thirst although his body boils inside his armour. It is there, so 'tis said, the lying priests consult their Oracle.'

'How far is it?'

'No man can say. It lies out in the unknown desert, that is all we know.'

'Cannot a guide be found?'

'They prefer to die in agony rather than speak.'

'But what of those who led us here from Memphis and Djebel Dakrour?'

'They will go no farther. They say their feet are tied and their lips are sealed by Ra.'

'Can no way be found to make them open them?'

'None – we have tried them all, you may be sure,' said Hystomannus dryly.

'Yet still we go?'

'Yet still. And now you know what I mean when I say that this is different.'

'I will go and sharpen my lance,' smiled Mazeus.

His father shook his head. 'The enemies that we shall have to face will not be those of flesh and blood. Didst ever see me flinch before stones or flying steel?'

'Never, my Father.'

'There are worse things in the wilderness: such things as thirst, heat, dust-devils that sweep across the sand and carry all before them. No sword can hold such things in play, no shield can stem their rush.'

'Father! It is not like you to talk this way,' cried Mazeus in alarm.

'I know, I know,' Hystomannus shook himself almost savagely. 'It is these accursed priests,' he muttered. 'We have destroyed their gods, and in the night strange voices say they will destroy us, too.'

Mazeus smiled, a little nervously, perhaps. 'We shall see. How many men are going on this expedition?'

'Fifty thousand.'

'You mean —?'

'The army marches forward as the sun goes down. Come, let us prepare.'

2. *The Desert Answers*

THUS, as the sun went down in a blaze of crimson glory, the mighty Persian host marched out in martial splendour: Parthian pikemen, Mardian archers, Scythian cavalry, Medes and Susians, slingers, bowmen, horse and foot, chariots and baggage-wagons – all moved out across the quivering dunes, confident of victory, never having known defeat.

Mazeus, with his lance at rest, rode beside his father near the royal wardrobe chest, which rested in a chariot beside the records of the historians who accompanied the king so that the story of his prowess might be told. Around this chariot rode the Royal Guard, drawn from the highest born in the noble city of Persepolis.

Swiftly the rim of the sun melted into the sand; the moon came up and a myriad stars blazed down from a sky of purple velvet, while along the line of marching men arose such sounds as the dunes had never heard before; the dull rumble of a hundred thousand feet, the musical jingle of arms and accoutrements, the creaking of wagons, the groans of toiling slaves, and the cracking of the whips of their task-masters.

For three long days and nights the army wound like a gigantic serpent across the brooding sand, halting when the sun was high, the soldiers seeking in vain for shelter where there was none; for not a tree, not a bird, not an animal or blade of grass, nor any other living thing broke the eternal monotony of sand, sand, and still more sand. Yet ever in the distance strange wraiths of smoke pointed upwards to the heavens like accusing fingers, while at night unearthly fire was seen to flicker in the dunes. And the marching men marched on in silence, avoiding each other's eyes, for in their hearts was fear.

On the evening of the third day, soon after the army had resumed its march, an excited murmur ran along the line. Hills could be seen ahead, so it was said, and the men were as cheered as ship-wrecked mariners when a coast is seen. Mazeus rode forward to the top of a towering dune and looked long and steadily at the line of jagged peaks, which, like a row of broken teeth, rose stark and clear into the sky. They were, he judged, still twenty miles away, but dawn should see the weary soldiers resting in their shade. He paused for a moment to watch the army winding through the sands, then he galloped back to his father to report.

It was nearly four hours later when he noticed, with more curiosity than alarm, that the moon had changed its colour. No longer was it an orb of gleaming silver; it had turned a creamy tint, almost golden; it appeared to be much larger, too, and misty at the edges. He called his father's attention to it, but all he got by way of answer was a curt 'Ride on!'

Another hour passed, and he saw that the moon had become a dullish, orange globe, a phenomenon he had never seen before. He noticed, too, that the pace of march had been increased, and that unusual noises now arose from the winding train behind. The crack of whips came faster, and the hoarse cries of the chariot-drivers were nearly drowned in the plaintive groaning of the camels. A breath of wind played for a moment on his cheek, but it brought him no refreshment, for it was as hot as if it had been breathed from the heart of a live volcano, and a thrill of apprehension swept through him.

'What means this speed, O Father?' he asked wonderingly, and then ran his tongue over his teeth, for there seemed to be some grit on them, which grated as he spoke.

'A storm is coming,' was the brief reply. 'Look at the moon.'

Mazeus turned, and caught his breath when he saw that it had turned dull brown, with edges blurred, as though a veil were being drawn across it. 'You mean a sand-storm?' he asked easily, for now he felt no fear, having seen such things before.

'Yes. Ride nearer to the chariot.'

'It will overtake us, you think, before we reach the hills?' questioned Mazeus, pressing his left leg against his horse's flank to move it nearer to the chariot.

'It will.'

'But we cannot be far away now.' As he spoke Mazeus turned again in the saddle, eyes seeking the moon, but now in vain. The column moved through a world of utter darkness.

'Tie your scarf across your mouth and keep close by my side,' his father told him, and a moment later came the wind.

At first it came quite quietly, a gentle sigh, a moan that crept across the wilderness; but then there came a gust, a howl, a searing, scorching blast, bringing with it a cloud of sand that stung and smarted like the bites of countless ants.

Mazeus bowed his head and swiftly tied his scarf about his mouth, at the same time fighting to check his plunging steed, in such darkness as he had never known. Where was the chariot? He moved, as he thought, towards it, but it was not where he had imagined it to be. Faintly, above the scream of the wind, he heard the groans of slaves and the cursing of the soldiers he could not see. Panic clutched his heart. Where was his father? 'Father!' he cried, but the blast, with a shriek of triumph, tore the word from his lips and flung it in the air. 'Father!' he called again, shortening his reins to control his frenzied mount. The animal, sensing his fear, reared high, then plunged. The rein snapped like a piece of cotton, and in an instant the maddened creature was racing before the storm.

Blindly, gasping for breath, Mazeus clung to the saddle with his left hand, still gripping in his right, perhaps from force of habit, his lance, for to lose a weapon in Cambyses' army meant, for the loser, death. And as he rode a thousand demons seemed to clutch him, tearing at his clothes, snatching at his body, scouring his face and hands with sand until they bled. Where he was going, in what direction, he did not know; he only knew that the sand was choking him to death; for he had to breathe, and every time he drew a breath, by nose or mouth, the tiny grains poured in and clogged his throat and lungs.

He was reeling in the saddle when the horse fell, with an almost human scream of terror. Thrown clear, he rose at once, groping for the animal. But it had gone. For a moment or two he stood still, appalled by the calamity, then he began to run. But he seemed to be staggering through a roaring tide which, snatching at his ankles, dragged him down. He fell, rose, and fell again, hardly knowing that he did. 'It is the end of the world,' he thought, in a vague, bewildered way as he blundered on only to fall again. This time he remained rigid, his questing hands feeling the earth beneath him. It was no longer sand. It was rock. He had reached the hills! Gradually, like a blind man on a strange road, he felt his way along it until he found the thing he sought, a cleft, a fault in the rocky *massif*, and into it he tumbled. The sand poured in, but it was not so bad as it was outside, and gradually the storm began to wane.

Came dawn, and he crawled wearily from his refuge, his face all raw and his dry lips cracked and bleeding. A dreadful thirst consumed him and he knew that he must drink or die. No longer could he remove the cloying sand from his mouth. The army? Yes, someone would see him when he raised his lance. Forcing open his aching eyes, he looked out across the desert, but all that met his gaze was sand, billowing yellow dunes of sand as far as the eye could see. Behind him was the mountain, grim and stark, as relentless as death itself. At first he did not understand. Where was the army? The thought repeated itself again and again in his reeling brain. Where could it have gone in so short a time? One thing alone was certain: it was not there.

He was not to know that nearly all the mighty Persian host, fifty thousand horse and foot, horses, carts, and chariots, lay buried in the sand not a mile from where he swayed, so that neither pike nor lance, wheel nor standard remained to mark its mile-square tomb.

'My father will come back,' he thought desperately. 'He will come back to seek me. I must make a mark that he will see. My lance!' Weakly, the dunes rocking before his eyes, he picked up the weapon and drove the handle deep into the sand, so that the point was skyward. This done, he lay down to wait.

The sun soared upwards, driving bars of living fire into the sterile earth. Silence reigned, the awful silence of the uttermost wilderness. The rays crept round the rock and played upon the huddled body that lay at the foot of the lance. It did not move. It would never move again, for the spirit of Mazeus, son of Hystomannus, the last survivor of Cambyses' Royal Guard, had gone to seek its comrades in the cloudless blue, above the eternal sand.

CHAPTER 1

THE MOONLIGHT ASSASSIN

Major James Bigglesworth, better known to his friends as Biggles, folded up the map he had been studying and put it on the paved terrace near the feet of the long cane-chair in which he was sitting.

'No,' he said, for the benefit of Ginger Hebblethwaite, who was standing near him. 'Quite definitely, no. Algy will bear me out – if he is capable of bearing anything – that when we started on this trip it was agreed that we should fly direct to Cape Town without any intermediate meandering. Yet here we are, rather less than half-way, and you want to fly off, literally, at a tangent. My answer is, unless any insuperable obstacle arises to prevent me from getting there, I am going to Cape Town and nowhere else.'

'Good enough, chief,' agreed Ginger, with just a hint of disappointment in his voice. 'It was only a suggestion, you know —'

'Yes, I know all about your suggestions. Say no more. The matter is closed.' Biggles settled back in his chair and reached for the iced drink that stood on a small table near his elbow.

'Picture of a Great White Chief putting his foot down,' murmured the Honourable Algernon Lacey, more often

19

known as Algy, catching Ginger's eye and smiling at his discomfiture.

The three airmen were in Egypt, where they had arrived a few days earlier after an uneventful flight from England in one of the new 'Tourer' twin-engined sports aeroplanes which had been acquired for the purpose.

The reason for the trip was quite a prosaic one. Major Mullen, Biggles's old C.O. in Number 266 Squadron, R.F.C., now a high official in South African civil aviation, had conceived the idea of a Squadron Reunion Dinner; but as many of the old members of the Squadron were now in Africa, in his service, it was decided that it would be more convenient for the majority if the dinner was held in Cape Town instead of London. This information, together with an invitation, had been sent to Biggles, who, having little to do at the time, had decided to accept, taking his two friends with him as guests. Naturally, it did not occur to him to travel any way other than by air, so a new machine had been purchased with the idea of making the occasion something of a pleasure cruise.

They had started with plenty of time at their disposal in order to make the journey in easy stages, which would allow them to see something of the places of interest on the route, and up to the time they reached Egypt this programme had been adhered to. They were now in Cairo, and had, in fact, been there for three days, leaving their machine at Heliopolis Aerodrome while they explored the ancient city.

Ginger, however, either because he found the slow progress somewhat irksome, or possibly because he was never so happy as when he was in the air, had lately formed a habit of suggesting minor expeditions by air, and it was such a proposal that he had just put forward. For reasons best known to himself – for he had not had time to disclose them – he had suddenly decided that he would like to see Jerusalem, and it was on this question that Biggles had given his decision.

They were staying at one of the lesser-known hotels on the outskirts of the city, partly because it was inexpensive, and partly because Biggles preferred to keep away from the usual tourist crowd with their clicking cameras and swarms of *baksheesh*-seeking natives. The hotel was, moreover, a small one, and they were not disappointed when they found that they had it almost to themselves. Night had fallen and they were sitting outside on the terrace under the gleaming Egyptian moon, enjoying a rest after a rather tiring day of 'seeing the sights'.

'So you're thinking of moving on tomorrow?' murmured Algy, glancing at Biggles.

'I think so. I fancy we have seen all that is likely to interest us here. We'll push on to Khartoum; there are one or two R.A.F. fellows stationed there whom I should like to look up.'

'Suits me,' agreed Algy. 'Anything for a quiet life. I find it curiously refreshing to be able to drift along like this, in our own time, instead of roaring about on some crazy business.'

Ginger wrinkled his nose but said nothing, and presently turned his attention to a particularly large white moth wheeling in erratic flight among the orange trees that stood at intervals in the garden, which began where the terrace ended. In many respects he was now grown up, but he had not yet lost the boyish desire to chase an attractive butterfly. Picking up his sun helmet in lieu of a net, and keeping as far as possible in the inky shadow of a group of fern-palms, he began a cautious advance towards his quarry; but he had not taken more than a dozen paces when he saw something that caused him to halt, tense and alert, the moth forgotten. Some twenty yards to his right a low white wall separated the garden from the road on which the hotel was situated; a line of tall date-palms followed the wall, and through their graceful fronds the moon cast a curious lattice-like pattern of black-and-white

bars that fell across the dappled flower-beds, the sandy
paths, and the wall beyond. Along the inside of the wall,
ghostly in the silvery half-light, was creeping the white-robed
figure of a native. The criss-cross shadows of the palm
fronds fell across his sheet-like *burnous* so that he appeared to
be gliding behind the bars of a cage; and so silent and furtive
were his movements that it was at once apparent that his
purpose was not a lawful one.

At this juncture it is probable that Ginger would have
denied that his interest was anything more than natural
curiosity. He had travelled far, and in strange lands, and the
mere unexpected appearance of a soft-footed native no longer
aroused in him the instinctive suspicion, and possible apprehension, that it does in most Europeans when first they find
themselves in a land where the native population is 'coloured'.
Yet there was at once something so sinister about the actions
of the intruder – for Ginger's common sense told him that the
man would not behave thus were he not trespassing – that he
felt his nerves tighten in expectation of something that was
about to happen.

Making no more noise than the object of his suspicion, he
took a pace or two nearer and placed his helmet on the
ground. A swift glance in the direction of the terrace revealed
Biggles and Algy still sitting where he had left them; the faint
murmur of their voices reached him, and he would have
attracted their attention had it been possible without alarming the man who was still creeping stealthily along the inside
of the wall. Reaching the wrought-iron gate that gave access
to the road from the garden, the intruder stopped, and it was
at that moment that Ginger had his first suspicion of his
purpose. He saw the moonlight glint dully on something that
he held in his right hand, and an instant later he heard footsteps beyond the wall, as though someone was approaching
the gate from the outside.

The inference was immediately apparent. A visitor was about to enter the hotel by the garden gate, and the man inside was stalking him with murderous intent.

Ginger, with the idea of frustrating this, at once started forward, and he was just in time to avert a tragedy. The garden gate swung inward, and a slim figure in European clothes, but wearing the customary *tarboosh* of the better-class Egyptian, appeared in the opening. At that moment the assassin made his attack, but Ginger, seeing what was about to happen, and perceiving that he could not reach the gate in time, had uttered a shout of warning; and there is no doubt that his prompt action saved the new-comer's life, for the cry had its effect on both actors in the drama. The figure in the *tarboosh* jumped aside, and his aggressor hesitated moment-arily in making his stroke.

By this time Ginger was less than half a dozen paces away, and his swift approach was heard. Even so, the assassin made a last desperate attempt to achieve his purpose; he made a cat-like spring, but the other was as quick, and warded off the gleaming blade by an upward sweep of his arm. The attacker, seeing that Ginger was now almost upon him, and noting, no doubt, that he was a white man, darted through the gate and fled.

Ginger, knowing the futility as well as the danger of pur-suit, did not attempt it, but contented himself with flinging a stone, which he snatched from the top of the wall, at the flying figure. It missed its mark, however, so with a grunt of chagrin he turned back to the gate, to find that Biggles and Algy had arrived on the scene.

'What's going on?' asked Biggles sharply.

'A fellow tried to knife this chap,' answered Ginger briefly, indicating the new-comer, who was standing near the wall with one arm resting against it. 'Jolly nearly got him, too,' he added, noting that the man he had saved was also a native.

Biggles's keen eyes evidently saw something that Ginger's did not, for he took a quick pace forward. 'Did he touch you?' he asked the stranger.

'It is nothing,' was the quiet answer, spoken in perfect English. 'My arm – a scratch – nothing more.'

'You had better come up into the light and let us have a look at it,' suggested Biggles in a friendly tone.

'Thank you. You are most kind,' was the soft answer, and the four of them walked quietly to the terrace.

'My word! You had a close squeak, and no mistake,' observed Biggles, as the stranger exhibited a slashed sleeve and a bloodstained hand. 'Algy, slip in and get a towel or something. Better ask the manager to come along, too.'

'No, say nothing,' put in the stranger quickly. 'It will be better so.'

'Well, it's your affair,' agreed Biggles as Algy hurried away on his errand.

While they were waiting for him to return Ginger had a good look at the man he had saved. He was, as he had already observed, a native, but obviously one of the better class, and his skin was not much darker than that of a sunburned white man. He was young, no older than himself, with finely cut features and soft, intelligent eyes. His clothes were of good quality, and might have been made in London; indeed, but for his distinguishing *tarboosh*, he might have passed for a European.

Algy soon returned with two soft linen face-towels. With one of these Biggles cleaned the wound, and with the other, folded in the manner of a bandage, he bound it up. Fortunately, as the victim had stated, it was little more than a scratch, and he smiled apologetically as Biggles gave him medical attention.

'Does this sort of thing often happen to you?' inquired Biggles. 'If it does, the sooner you provide yourself with a suit of armour, or a bodyguard, the better. You might not be so lucky next time.'

'It has never happened to me before,' was the candid reply.

'Are you feeling all right now?' Biggles asked the question in a manner which suggested politely that the wounded man was free to proceed on his errand if he so wished.

'Quite all right, thanks to you,' was the quiet answer. But the stranger made no move to depart.

There was rather an embarrassing silence in which Biggles lit a cigarette.

'You were coming to the hotel, weren't you?' inquired Ginger, more for the sake of saying something than inquisitiveness.

The answer took them all by surprise. 'Yes, I was coming to see you,' said the young Egyptian quietly, looking at Biggles.

'To see *me*?' Biggles was frankly astonished.

'Yes – you are Major Bigglesworth, are you not?'

Biggles looked at their guest with renewed interest. 'Yes, that is my name,' he admitted. 'Sit down if you have something to tell me.'

'Thanks. I will, if you don't mind. The shock of the attack has left me a little – how do you say? – shaken.'

There was another short silence while the visitor seated himself, and the airmen waited for him to continue.

'My name is Kadar Alloui Bey,' he said at last, in a manner which suggested that it might mean something to his listeners.

Biggles shook his head. 'Do not think me discourteous, but I am afraid I must confess that your name means nothing to me.'

'No – of course, you are a stranger here. My father's name is not unknown in Cairo.'

'I see,' returned Biggles awkwardly. 'You came to see me about something?' he prompted.

'Yes. The circumstances of my arrival have made my mission rather difficult, but – you are an air pilot, I believe?'

'That is correct,' admitted Biggles, wondering what was coming next.

The other coughed nervously. 'I was coming here to ask you if you would care to sell me your aeroplane.'

Biggles stared. 'Sell you my aeroplane?' he repeated wonderingly.

'Yes, I have urgent need of one.'

'But couldn't you get one here – I mean, through the usual channels? Haven't Misr Airwork got one for disposal?'

'No, unfortunately. As far as I can discover there is not an aeroplane for sale in Egypt – at least, not of the sort I require. You see, I need a large one, and all the large ones are in use on the air routes. Owing to the air expansion in England there are no civil aeroplanes to spare; even the air line companies need more than they have, for they are running to capacity on every service.'

'I see. Well, I'm afraid we need ours. In any case, do you know what an aeroplane costs?' Biggles asked the question seriously, feeling sure that the young Egyptian must be unaware of the cost of a large modern aeroplane, and that when he was better informed he would soon give up the idea of buying one.

'A twin-engined tourer such as yours costs, I believe, eight thousand pounds. Had you been here on business I was prepared to offer ten thousand pounds for it,' was the calm answer.

Biggles could hardly believe his ears. 'You are right about the price,' he confessed. 'Still, I am afraid I cannot part with my machine. All the same, we are in no great hurry, and if you want a lift somewhere it might be arranged. In fact,

under certain conditions, if your purpose is really urgent –
which apparently it is – I would be prepared to let you
charter it for a couple of days.'

The other shook his head and smiled as he stood up.
'Thank you. That is very generous of you, but I am afraid
that would be no use. I should need it for some time, and it
might take me a little while to find a pilot.'

'I see. You can't fly yourself?'

'No. I was in rather a difficult position. It was no use my
engaging a pilot before I had an aeroplane. Had I been able
to buy one, my intention was then to find a pilot to fly it for
me, to take me to the place I wish to visit.'

'I understand,' said Biggles slowly. 'I am sorry, but I am
afraid we can't do anything about it. As a matter of detail,
we are on our way to Cape Town. If your objective lies in that
direction, we shall be happy to give you a lift.'

'No, I fear that would not do, thank you all the same,'.
answered the young Egyptian rather sadly. 'I am sorry to
have taken up your time. Never mind; perhaps it would be
better if I abandoned my project.'

A new thought struck Biggles. 'Was the project you mention the reason for the attack made on you just now?'

'Undoubtedly,' was the instant reply. 'I think it would be
safe to say that it was in order to prevent my reaching you
that I was waylaid. There could be no other reason. I knew I
was being watched, but I did not think my enemies would go
as far as to try to murder me.'

'Somebody must be very anxious to keep you in Cairo,'
smiled Biggles.

'Yes, very anxious, and I think I know who it is. But there,
as I say, no doubt he will leave me alone when it becomes
known that I have abandoned my proposed quest.'

The final word made Ginger prick up his ears. 'Quest?'
The word was a naïve question.

Biggles frowned. 'Don't be inquisitive,' he admonished him.

Their guest smiled. 'It is no secret,' he said. 'Yes, I suppose one would call it a quest. I have spent some years preparing for it, so it is rather disappointing to have to give it up. Still, we must learn to accept these things as they come.'

'You speak English very well,' said Biggles, changing the subject.

'That is not surprising, considering that I was at school in England for seven years,' was the unexpected reply.

'The dickens you were!'

'What was this quest you were projecting?' persisted Ginger.

'I am afraid it is rather a long story.'

'Well, the night is young,' declared Biggles. 'I can't make any promises, but if you feel like telling us something more about it, perhaps —'

'I will tell you with pleasure, because I know without being told that you will respect my confidence. Much of my information is common property, but there are some things —'

'Shall we sit down and have some coffee?' suggested Biggles.

'Thank you, you are most hospitable.'

'Ring the bell, Ginger,' ordered Biggles.

CHAPTER 2

KADAR'S STORY

WHEN they were all comfortably settled and a native servant had placed coffee on a brass-topped table between them, Biggles looked at their guest. 'Go ahead,' he invited.

The young Egyptian leaned forward, his dark eyes keen with eagerness. 'In the first place,' he began, 'as I tell my story I want you to bear in mind two things: one is that this subject on which I am going to speak has a peculiar fascination for me – I mention that to account for what may seem a disproportionate enthusiasm on my part. Secondly, my father was, until he retired a few years ago, an honorary assistant curator of antiquities at the Cairo Museum, where, as you probably know, the most famous relics of ancient Egypt are kept. Naturally, he taught me much, and that is why I am well informed on a subject which, to most people, is of no importance. Have you ever heard of the Lost Oasis?'

'Vaguely,' answered Biggles, wrinkling his forehead.

'I know a little about it,' put in Ginger, somewhat to the others' surprise.

'How did you learn about it?' inquired Biggles curiously.

'I remember reading something about it in a paper called *Popular Flying*,' explained Ginger.

'That is correct. I read the article myself,' declared Kadar Alloui. 'In fact, I cut it out, and have it here in my pocket. It deals with the last attempt to locate the oasis, the expedition being made by air. I think it would be a good thing if I read it to you, because that will tell you, more or less officially, how the matter has been left. But before doing that I must ask another question. It is not necessarily associated with the Lost Oasis, but – well, it may be. One must consider both questions to gather the full significance of my proposed quest. Did you, when you were at school, or since, hear the name Cambyses?'

'Wasn't he a general who got lost in the desert, or something of the sort?' answered Biggles.

'Yes. That is more or less correct, but what actually happened was this. In the year 525 BC, Cambyses, the son of Cyrus, the founder of the great Persian Empire – the greatest empire in the world at that time – conquered Egypt. He destroyed the Egyptian gods, and, to complete all, he decided to plunder Jupiter Ammon, a famous sanctuary situated near the Oasis of Siwah. I must tell you about this temple of Ammon, which was then the centre of the great Ammonite kingdom. At the time of which we are speaking, and for many centuries later, it was the most celebrated place of pilgrimage in the world, on account of its Oracle. In other words, the high priests claimed to be able to tell the fortunes of those who went there to consult them. Many people still believe in fortune-tellers, so it is not hard to imagine that the Temple of Ammon flourished in those superstitious days. Everyone believed in its power, and everyone who could afford it went there to learn his fate. You must understand that it was not then so inaccessible as it is now. It stood at the cross-roads of the two great African caravan trails – perhaps the oldest roads in the world. Alexander the Great went there to consult the Oracle. So did Hannibal, the famous Carthaginian general: he made a special journey there to ask what would happen if he made war on the Romans. Croesus, the man of fabulous wealth, went there, as did many other kings and princes. This, then, was the shrine that Cambyses proposed to plunder, and we need not wonder why. There must have been vast wealth stored there; indeed, there are still many legends of treasures hidden beneath the crumbling stones.'

'Then it is still there?' put in Biggles.

'Oh yes, although the temple is now in ruins. But we will return to that presently. Cambyses' army left the Oasis of Khargah, but it never reached Ammon. Nothing more was ever heard of it. Not a man returned. That night the army disappeared as completely as if the earth had opened and swallowed it up – as indeed, in a way, no doubt it did. And this brings us to the Lost Oasis, named, some say, Zenzura.

'Whether or not this Oasis really exists no man can say, yet it would be a strange thing, would it not, if a name could exist without foundation? From time to time through the ages there have come out of the desert strange rumours of an Oasis, and ruined cities, far away in the heart of the dreaded Libyan sands, known to the Tuareg Arabs as the Region of Devils. If you will look at a map of Africa you will see that all that area is left white, without a mark of any sort on it, unless it be the intriguing word "unknown". Certainly no white man has ever crossed it. Yet rumours of a mysterious oasis have persisted, and that is not all. The Tuaregs, the cruel nomads of the desert, even tell of a strange white race that live there. If that seems hard to believe, remember that there is a race of white Arabs farther west, in the heart of the Sahara, the descendants, it is generally believed by scientists of a lost party of Phoenicians. As you probably know, the Phoenician civilization of North Africa was one of the greatest in the early days of the world. When, as I say, one remembers this, there would not appear to be any reason why, if there is an oasis far out in the desert, it should not be peopled by the descendants of the survivors of Cambyses' ill-fated army. Whatever the disaster was that overwhelmed it, one would expect some to escape, possibly the scouts or advance guards. If some of these did, in fact, reach an oasis in the heart of the great sands, they would have to remain there. It would be impossible for them to get back to civilization. They would be marooned more effectively than mariners on a desert island. On an island there is always a chance, however remote, that a ship will one day call, but the fiery heart of the Libyan Desert is perhaps the one place on earth where no one has ever gone, or is likely to go. There could be no hope of rescue, for not even the most daring explorer would venture there. It is rock, sand, and desolation un-utterable. Nothing more. It never rains —'

'You don't mean that literally, do you?' interrupted Biggles.

'It is hardly a misstatement,' was the firm reply. 'The people who live on the fringe of the sands say that no rain has fallen there for more than three hundred years.'

'Not exactly the spot to open a barometer shop,' remarked Ginger.

Kadar saw no humour in the observation. 'It would be a bad place,' he said seriously. 'From day to day, from month to month, and from year to year, you can always be quite sure that tomorrow will be as yesterday; cloudless, and of such heat as is scarcely possible to imagine. What would you call a hot day in England?'

'A shade temperature of about eighty degrees Fahrenheit is reckoned to be hot,' answered Biggles. 'Ninety degrees is a rarely experienced heat-wave.'

'Then try to imagine what *a hundred and fifty degrees* in the shade would be like – that is, if there *was* any shade.'

'Phew!' exclaimed Ginger.

'This doesn't happen to be the place you propose visiting, I hope?' murmured Biggles dryly.

'Yes, this is the place.'

'I see,' nodded Biggles. 'Go on. What about that cutting you were going to read?'

Kadar took out his note-case, selected a clipping from among several, and smoothed out the creases. 'This article is entitled "The Lost Oasis, or, Has Aviation Solved an Age-Old Riddle of the Sands?" ' he continued. 'The early part of it deals with the historical facts which I have already given you. It goes on to say:

"Quite recently Sir Robert Clayton and Mr L. E. de Almasy carried out a flight of exploration in a Moth over this region, and discovered what may prove to be the Lost Oasis of Zenzura. They were accompanied by Mr P. A. Clayton, of the Egyptian Government Desert Survey, and Squadron-Leader Penderel, R.A.F., in a Vickers Victoria twin-engined Troop Carrier. They made their base at Khargah Oasis (from which Cambyses' ill-fated army set forth) and flew over a large plateau known as Gilf el Kebir, in the direction of Kufra. Khargah is about three hundred and seventy-five miles south of Cairo.

"Running eastwards through this plateau, Sir Robert and his companions sighted a large and fertile *wadi*, or valley. Photographs were taken from the air, and enlargements distinctly show a white spot among the trees which is believed to be a hut. This discovery suggests that the *wadi* was recently inhabited, and tends to confirm the belief that it is identical with the Lost Oasis of Zenzura."

'The rest of the article,' continued Kadar, 'consists of a narrative by Sir Robert Clayton setting out particulars of the ground organization. He concludes by saying:

' "Although we were able to fly over what we considered to be our object, we were forced to return to our base three days later, as the expedition had been timed to turn back on that day and no further supplies had been provided."

'The remainder of the article deals only with the prospects of future expeditions,' concluded Kadar, looking up from the paper.

'What date was that?' asked Biggles.

'It was some time ago,' replied Kadar. 'The article appeared in the August 1932 issue of the paper, so presumably the expedition was just before that time.'

'And this was the sort of trip you were hoping to make?' suggested Biggles.

'Yes,' confessed Kadar, folding up the cutting and putting it back into his pocket.

'How exactly did you propose to go about it?'

'I am coming to that,' answered Kadar. 'Ever since I was a small boy the problem of the Lost Oasis has fascinated me. Can you wonder? Even if the Oasis does not exist, somewhere out in the sands lies the mummified remains of an army, with its weapons, armour, chariots and baggage, just as it took the field nearly two thousand five hundred years ago. What a find that would be for an archaeologist – or anyone else, for that matter, since there is certain to be much of value there. And that brings me, I suspect, to the reason for the attack made on me just now. You will believe me, I hope, when I say that my interest is entirely in the historical aspect, and that it was solely in the hope of throwing fresh light on the world's history that my father agreed to finance an expedition into the desert – not necessarily by air, of course. I have only contemplated that during the last few days. But the question of possible wealth hidden in the sands is not to be ignored. Legend has it that the chariot carrying

Cambyses' treasure-chest was lost with the army, and, frankly, I think it is more than likely that it was. Be that as it may, from time to time jewels – mostly uncut emeralds and rubies – have reached Cairo and Alexandria from a mysterious source. They appear to pass through several hands, and no one knows where they come from. You will agree, I think, that it would not be straining the imagination very hard to suspect that they are coming out of the desert, and that the source is either Jupiter Ammon or the final resting-place of the Persian host. It was in the hope of being able to learn something about this fount of wealth that I have made three journeys into the desert, in disguise, for should my supposition prove correct, then I should soon be on the trail of things far more important to me than mere money.'

'Did you gather any information?' asked Biggles, almost eagerly.

'A little. My task was a difficult one. You see, I know the Bedouin too well to make the fatal mistake of asking questions. But they are born gossipers – as is only natural, for they have no other means of spreading information – and I hoped, by listening, to pick up any rumours that were current concerning the mysterious jewels, the lost army, or the Lost Oasis. As I say, I learned a little, and it may have been due to the fact that I made no secret of it that my plans have now miscarried.'

'Is it expecting too much to ask what you discovered?' inquired Biggles.

'Not in the least,' was the frank reply. 'Actually, all I discovered in substance was an inscription on a stone, the existence of which was reported to me by a friendly Bedouin who suspected my mission. I did not see the stone myself, for I was not equipped for such a journey as would have been entailed, but he went out and made a copy of it on paper. Inscribed stones, ruined buildings, and aqueducts occur over the whole of what is now the Libyan and Saharan deserts, relics of the great civilizations that existed there in the dim past; but one glance at the inscription brought to me by the Arab was enough to excite me, for the characters were cuneiform letters. A translation told me that the Persian army had actually passed the spot where the stone was found. That was one thing. The second item of importance was a story told to me by a very old man at the Oasis of Siwah. He said he was more than a hundred years old, and it may have been true. He told me that when he was a young man he was out on a raid, and in the darkness of the night he became lost. He was lost for three days. On the second day, by which time he was suffering greatly from thirst, he saw a spear, or lance, of a type which he had never seen before, sticking up out of the sand near some barren hills. The handle was made of a dark-coloured wood unknown to him and reinforced with carved brasswork.'

'Did he collect it?' asked Biggles.

'Unfortunately, no. Such was his plight that the last thing he thought of was to burden himself further, so he left the lance where it was, intending to return for it later should he manage to get back to his friends. He did, in fact, get back, but the tribe shortly afterwards moved its tents so that he had no opportunity of fetching the lance. Still, it is something to know it is there, for where there is one it is more than likely there will be others. The description given by the Arab makes it almost certain that the lance was of Persian origin. What is even more important is that the two clues, the inscribed stone and the lance, give me the Persian line of march.'

'So the Arab told you where the lance could be found – or where he saw it?'

'Yes, as far as description is possible in the desert, where there is seldom anything to describe. Fortunately, as I have told you, the weapon happened to be at the base of some rocky hills, so that should greatly facilitate a search. And, I may say, the area is the one through which Cambyses' army might easily have marched; that is to say, it is not far south of a straight line taken between Khargah and Jupiter Ammon. You will remember that Khargah was the point of departure, and Jupiter Ammon, which is close to the Oasis of Siwah, the objective.'

'This Oasis of Siwah?' queried Biggles. 'Is it inhabited?'

'Certainly.'

'Are the people savage?' asked Ginger curiously.

'They are not exactly friendly, but one would not call them dangerous. Until recently it would have been certain death for a stranger, particularly a Christian, to go there. All the explorers who reached the place in the last century were ill-treated; in fact, few escaped with their lives. But allow me to return to the matter of this information which I discovered, for the most important development is yet to come.

'On all my journeyings, sooner or later I came up against what I can only describe by using the French word *impasse*. I could get no farther. Something was there, I felt, but it ever escaped me. At first I put it down to a natural reticence on the part of the Arabs, but in the end I became convinced that it was organized opposition to my plans; and this was borne out in a curious way when, not long ago, I announced my definite intention to proceed.' Kadar broke off and glanced around nervously. When he resumed he did so in a low voice.

'A man came to see me,' he went on softly. 'He is a man well known in Cairo, affluent and influential. He is neither English nor Egyptian. He is, I think, half Turkish and half Greek – but that does not really matter. He came to see me and, much to my surprise, offered to finance my expedition under certain conditions, which were, briefly, that we should retain for our own use anything of value that we discovered. Naturally, I would have nothing to do with such a proposal, which was, not to mince words, dishonest. I must explain, in case you do not know, that every antiquity now found in Egypt becomes automatically the property of the Government, which is only right and proper, or Egypt would soon be denuded of the treasures of her romantic past. Most of the finds go into the museum here in Cairo, or Alexandria; some are distributed to other museums, such as your British Museum in London. Naturally, the finder is recompensed for his trouble. So now you see how distasteful this man's proposal was to me. In any case, I do not like him. He is not a man whom one could trust. Well, that was all. He went away and I heard no more, but I have felt a sinister influence opposing all my plans. My own opinion is, although I would not dare to say this in public, that Zarwan – his name is Fuad Zarwan, by the way – is behind these jewel finds. He finances the Tuareg, and then, from a secret source, bring him what they find.'

'A profitable business,' murmured Biggles.

'Very profitable indeed,' agreed Kadar. 'But to conclude. The affair took rather a disconcerting turn the other night when all my notes and plans were stolen. Actually, the loss was not vital because I had memorized everything, but it means that whoever stole my plans and notes now knows as much as I do. It was possibly in order to make himself the sole possessor of the information that the thief attempted to take my life.'

'Well, this is all very interesting,' said Biggles quietly. 'Your idea was originally, I take it, to lead an expedition into this mysterious land in search of the Lost Oasis?'

'Yes, the Oasis was my chief objective, firstly to settle any doubt as to whether or not there is such a place, and if there is, to try to discover if the inhabitants – if there are any – are descendants of the survivors of Cambyses' army. Failing to find the Oasis, I hoped to find the spot where the Persian army perished. But my plans having been stolen, assuming that the thief would try to take advantage of his knowledge, it seemed to me that my only chance of reaching the spot first would be to fly there.'

'You do not mean that you hoped to fly straight there and back?'

'Oh, no. I should establish a base at Semphis, which is a small, uninhabited oasis to the west of the large oasis of Dakhel, on the fringe of the great desert. It lies between Kkargah and Ammon, and must be on, or near, the line of march of Cambyses' army.'

'What about petrol and stores? Quite a lot of things would be required.'

'My intention was to send a caravan on with them to Semphis. Having established a base there, I could then explore the surrounding country at leisure.'

'Such an organization would cost a lot of money,' declared Biggles dubiously.

'My father was prepared to finance me. He is as interested as I am, and he is not a poor man.' Kadar made the statement quietly, without any hint of pride or vanity.

'I see.' Biggles stroked his chin thoughtfully while Ginger watched him expectantly. Algy lit a cigarette.

The young Egyptian stood up. 'Well, I must be returning home,' he announced. 'My father will be wondering what has become of me.'

'Just a minute.' There was a peculiar smile on Biggles's face as he said the words. 'Your story has interested me very much indeed. I am always sorry to see thieves get away with anything. Let me think about this. Perhaps we shall be able to come to some arrangement after all. Come back in the morning and I will give you my views on it.'

CHAPTER 3

ZARWAN CALLS

AFTER Kadar had gone Algy turned an accusing eye on Biggles. 'I thought we were going straight to Cape Town,' he scoffed.

Biggles smiled. 'To tell you the honest truth, I was very much taken with that lad's story,' he confessed. 'I liked his straightforward manner, too. This delving into the dark pages of history is extremely fascinating, and it would be rather gratifying to contribute something to archaeological research – quite apart from which there would be some satisfaction in doing the thieves who stole the lad's plans out of what they hope to gain.'

'And get knifed for our trouble,' growled Algy. 'We seem to do nothing but dash about the world crashing into other people's affairs. This trip will cost a pretty penny, I imagine.'

'The boy's father will pay expenses, no doubt. You heard what he said. If it costs us nothing, as we have a little time on our hands —'

'You've decided to go?'

'I haven't definitely made up my mind yet.'

Algy yawned. 'Well, I suppose we may as well go there as anywhere,' he agreed. 'I've always wanted to have a look at the inside of a real, first-class desert.'

'If we go with this lad you're likely to get your wish,'

Biggles told him. 'Pass me that map, will you? I'd like to get an idea of where this place —' He broke off abruptly, staring at a man who was standing near them on the terrace. So quiet had been his arrival that Biggles had no idea of his presence; nor could he imagine how he had appeared without being heard.

The others had turned at Biggles's unaccountable silence, and, seeing the man standing there, Algy got up belligerently, for if there was one thing he could not tolerate it was eaves-dropping.

Apparently the new-comer sensed this in his manner, for he moved forward into the light, revealing himself to be a middle-aged man of undoubted eastern extraction notwith-standing the fact that he was dressed in expensive European clothes. He was short and inclined to corpulency, but this in no way impeded his movements, for they were made with the smooth grace of a cat. His skin was dark, as were his eyes, which, like those of many orientals, appeared to be heavy and curiously expressionless. He was clean-shaven, and his regular although somewhat rounded features might almost have justified his being described as good-looking; but there was something smugly self-satisfied and well-fed about his expression, and, as Algy afterwards put it, one felt that if one stroked him he would purr. He was, in fact, of a type common in the Middle East, where east and west are all too often blended with unfortunate results.

Biggles spoke first. 'Are you looking for me, by any chance?' he asked curtly.

The man bowed, and his right hand touched his heart with an obsequious gesture. 'Have I the honour of addressing the celebrated Major Bigglesworth?' he inquired suavely.

'My name is Bigglesworth, if that's what you mean,' answered Biggles coldly.

'Ah! Permit me to present myself. Fuad Zarwan, Esquire,

at your service.' As the man spoke he bowed again in a manner that made Biggles long to kick him. 'I fear with deep regret that your privacy has been disturbed tonight,' he continued smoothly.

'Even if it has, I do not see that you have any cause either for fear or regret,' Biggles told him frankly.

The man moved nearer. 'Pardon me, sirs,' he almost crooned.

'What precisely is your business here?' asked Biggles in no uncertain manner.

'I have come to express my deep regret at the inconvenience you have suffered.'

'I have suffered no inconvenience, and, if I had, I cannot see that you need lose any sleep on that account,' said Biggles in a manner that would have settled an argument with an Englishman there and then.

But the Turko-Greek only smiled and took out a heavy gold cigarette-case, at the same time, with studied careless-ness, allowing the light to fall on an enormous diamond ring which he wore on a rather podgy finger. 'Will you smoke?' he murmured.

If by this ostentatious display of wealth he expected to impress Biggles he was sadly in error, for the result was the reverse. And his next words, after Biggles had refused the proffered case, did nothing to calm Biggles's rising spleen.

'It is very sad about that unfortunate young man who came to see you tonight,' he observed, placing his fingers together in an attitude of prayer.

'Why sad?' asked Biggles crisply, yet not without curiosity.

The other extended the palms of his hands. 'To be insane is an unhappy state.'

'Ah!' murmured Biggles. 'I see. So he is insane?'

'At least, he suffers from strange delusions.'

'About things like lost oases?'

'Exactly.'

'Are you his guardian or something?' asked Biggles.

'No, but we do not like to see visitors – I might say guests – in our country molested by such people.'

'Just as a matter of interest, how do you know he came here to molest me?' inquired Biggles.

The other hesitated for a moment. Then he shrugged his shoulders. 'Well, you see —'

'Yes, I think I see very clearly,' said Biggles softly. Not for one moment did he believe that there was anything wrong with the young Egyptian.

'Good! I am glad,' declared Zarwan. 'You will take no further notice of his foolish ramblings, I hope?'

'None whatever,' answered Biggles with a curious smile.

The other's manner changed suddenly. 'Of course, if you seek adventure, and would like to take part in an expedition, no doubt it could be arranged.'

'You are sending one somewhere, then?'

The other nodded. 'Yes,' he said, 'and an aeroplane would perhaps be useful.'

Biggles hesitated. He had, of course, no intention of accepting the man's offer, or even considering it, but he was trying to work out the wisest policy to pursue. There was no point in deliberately making an enemy of the man, if, by pretending to play into his hands, there was a chance that he might learn something. Yet a moment's reflection was enough to convince him that such a course was unthinkable. He could not associate with a man whose very presence was distasteful. In the end he compromised. 'We are on our way to Cape Town,' he said casually. 'We shall be leaving in a day or two.'

The other bowed. 'Perhaps you are wise,' he murmured.

Biggles frowned. Even if he made an enemy of him he was

not prepared to accept threats from such a man. 'Just what do you mean by that?' he asked coldly.

The half-caste, with a natural but significant movement, put his hand into his breast pocket and allowed it to remain there. 'Visitors in Egypt are well advised not to become inquisitive in matters that do not concern them,' he said softly.

Again Biggles hesitated, controlling an urge to kick the man off the terrace. 'I gather that it would annoy you if we took part in another expedition.'

'It would be imprudent of you to take part in an expedition that might interfere with my own.'

Biggles kept control of himself by an effort. 'I see,' he said smiling, but there was no humour in his eyes. 'I'll bear it in mind.'

Zarwan bowed. 'It is a great relief to hear you say that,' he said glibly. 'With your permission I will now withdraw, regretting the necessity for troubling you.' He held out his hand, but Biggles was busy lighting a cigarette.

When he looked up the man had gone, so he flicked aside the spent match and turned to Algy. 'You will go a long way before you meet a nastier piece of work than that,' he said quietly. 'Did you notice the whites of his eyes? They were yellow, like those of a wolf, and never by any chance did he look any one of us straight in the face.'

'Why didn't you kick the oily-faced hog into the road?' demanded Algy hotly. 'I would have done.'

'And spent the rest of our stay in Egypt preventing people from sticking knives into us,' replied Biggles calmly. 'Oh, no. I should say that that gentleman is a knife-thrower in a big way. There was no sense in precipitating an exhibition of it; that will come soon enough, if I know my man.'

'What do you mean?'

'I mean,' answered Biggles, 'if it is all the same to you, I am going with our young Egyptian friend to help him to find Cambyses and his merry men – or what is left of them.'

'When are you going to start – tomorrow?' asked Ginger eagerly.

Biggles smiled. 'I shouldn't think so. As they have been lost for about twenty-five hundred years, a day or two more or less shouldn't make much difference. But what about a spot of bed? It must be getting late.'

CHAPTER 4

A DISCONCERTING DISCOVERY

FROM a height of nearly ten thousand feet Biggles looked down on a land that was old when Cambyses came to it.[1] The Nile and its clustering rice fields with their irrigation ditches had long been left behind; the groups of palms and scattered settlements had become more and more widely parted, and now the open desert lay ahead.

Nearly three weeks had elapsed since Kadar had escaped death in the garden of the hotel in Cairo, and for the little party of explorers they had been busy ones. On the morning following the affair in the hotel garden Biggles had announced his willingness to undertake the flight with Kadar provided his father was prepared to pay the expenses involved, and to this the learned Egyptian professor had readily agreed. The expenses, it transpired, were not so heavy on account of the air journey – since they already had an aircraft – as for the ground organization. Fuel and stores would be required at the proposed base at Semphis, and, quite apart from their original cost, there was the question of transport. As it happened, Kadar's plans in this respect were already made, so, three days after Biggles's decision, a caravan had departed

[1] Egypt had been a kingdom for over 1,600 years when it was conquered by Cambyses in 525 BC.

46

for the rendezvous, taking such things as would be required for a two or three weeks' stay. Relieved of this responsibility, the airmen were free to make their plans, and with these they had been able to proceed carefully, for it was proposed not to start until the caravan had reached, or nearly reached, its destination. There would, of course, be no point in their doing so, for in any case they would have to await the arrival of the extra fuel before undertaking any long-distance flights.

Nothing more had been seen or heard of Zarwan, much to Biggles's surprise and relief, for, knowing the type of man he was dealing with, he was fully prepared for him to cause mischief; but in the circumstances it could only be assumed that his veiled threat had merely been bluff to try to prevent Biggles and his companions becoming interested in Kadar's undertaking. Nevertheless, they were on their guard, for Kadar was convinced that the attempt on his life had been instigated by his crafty rival. There was, however, he explained, just a slight chance that the attack had been planned by someone else. There was in Egypt, he told them, a religious sect opposed to anything in the nature of exploration; but their activities had hitherto been directed against the mercenaries who did not hesitate to despoil tombs, or even violate the bodies of the dead, for monetary gain; and in view of his sincere pursuit of knowledge he thought it most unlikely that they would offer him violence or attempt to thwart his plans.

Only one point worried Biggles, and that was the matter of landing in the desert, or coming down at other than a recognized aerodrome. While they were on the great Imperial Airways southern route down Africa, which they had followed as far as Assiut, this did not arise, but thereafter any landing was bound to be subject to a certain amount of risk. Without landing there was no means of ascertaining what the surface of the ground was like, and there was, in fact, no way

of overcoming this difficulty. Biggles did not forget that while
firm sand provided an excellent surface, soft sand can be fatal
to an aeroplane. The machine can land, provided the sand is
not too soft, but it cannot take off again, the reason being that
the wheels sink into the ground and get clogged, which pre-
vents the aeroplane getting sufficient flying speed to rise – as
more than one unlucky pilot has discovered to his cost. Soft
snow acts in very much the same way.

This, then, was Biggles's chief concern as he left the main air
route at Assiut and, turning westward, headed out over the
open desert towards the rendezvous at Semphis. They saw
nothing of the caravan, nor did they expect to, for it was
coming from another direction, via Siwah Oasis, over what
is generally supposed to have been Alexander the Great's line
of march.

So far the journey had been uneventful and comparatively
simple. The travellers had done most of their flying in the
early hours of the morning, which is the best time for flying
in Egypt, as the air is apt to become very bumpy during the
heat of the day.

On this, their final long run to Semphis, they had started
before dawn in the hope of reaching their objective before the
real heat of the midday sun made flying uncomfortable. And
in this they were successful, for, shortly after the machine
began to climb what seemed to be a series of invisible waves,
the oasis crept up over the horizon – much to Biggles's relief,
for on such a flight a slight error of judgement, or in the
compass, might have tragic results.

On all sides lay the desert, a wilderness of sand, grim,
stark, silent, and relentless: a place of death. No wonder the
Tuareg, the fierce, veiled warriors of the desert, called it the
Region of Devils, thought Ginger, as he regarded it through
the cabin window with inward misgivings. As far as the eye
could see stretched the sand; it seemed incredible that there

could be so much. For the most part it was flat, or slightly undulating, but farther to the south it lay in great piled-up dunes, some with curling crests, like a yellow, storm-tossed sea suddenly arrested in motion. From time to time the dunes appeared to quiver as if the merciless sun, from a sky of steely blue, tormented them with its fiery rays.

Ginger shivered suddenly in spite of the heat, and turning his eyes, looked out ahead. In the clear, dry atmosphere the oasis could be seen from a great distance, how far he was able to judge from the fact that it took the Tourer nearly half an hour to reach it.

Biggles was watching the belt of palm-trees closely. As he had been given to expect, there was no sign of life, so after circling once or twice in order to try to pick out the most suitable place for a landing, he throttled back and began to glide down. If he felt any qualms he showed none, but secretly he was more than a little relieved when the wheels bumped slightly on hard ground and the machine ran to a standstill on the western edge of the fairly extensive group of palms.

Nothing, except possibly a South Sea island, lives up to its reputation more than an oasis in a desert. It is all that has been written and said of it, and the Oasis of Semphis was no exception; so it was, therefore, with considerable satisfaction that Biggles taxied the machine into the deepest shade of the palms and switched off the engines.

'Well, here we are,' he announced. 'Let's get out and stretch our legs. Phew! It's warm, isn't it? I think a little refreshment would not come amiss.'

They got out, but before doing anything else they all assisted in covering the engines, the fuselage, and the wings with the dark-green covers which had been brought for the purpose, both as a protection against the sun, and to prevent the sand from silting in. This applied particularly to the

engines. This done, they quenched their thirst, and then proceeded to make camp, or rather, prepare a site, with such
limited stores as they had at their disposal. This was soon
done, and, the task completed, they settled down to await the
arrival of the caravan.

Biggles fetched his maps, and, in close conference with
Kadar, checked up the marks he had made on it, one of
which, covering a fairly large area, was the most likely site of
the Lost Oasis of Zenzura. Ginger, however, was soon tired
of watching this; his restless spirit chafed at the delay, so he
decided to pass the time by exploring the oasis. Algy, having
nothing better to do, went with him.

It was not a very exciting pastime. The oasis was, as nearly
as they could judge it, between two and three miles long and
about half a mile wide, but there was a tiresome monotony
about it. On the outskirts it began with straggling date-palms,
their sun-scorched boles rising straight out of the sand. The
trees became closer together, however, and taller in habit,
with frequent pendant clusters of fruit, as they neared the
depression in the centre where the much-trampled water-hole
was situated. Round it for some distance grew a kind of
coarse grass, and in one place a fearsome growth of prickly
pear raised its thick, lozenge-shaped foliage, studded with
small scarlet fruits. That was all. The heat, even in the shade,
was intense, and the two wanderers were soon glad to rejoin
the others. Ginger, still restless, walked over to the machine,
ostensibly to make sure that the dust-covers were secure, but
in reality simply for something to do.

Satisfied that the covers would not move if there came a
wind, he was about to turn away when his nostrils caught the
faint but unmistakable smell of petrol. Standing quite still,
wondering whether he should call Biggles, he distinctly heard
a slight *phut*. He was on his hands and knees instantly,
crawling under the centre of the fuselage, from where the

sound had seemed to come. Nor was he mistaken. A few seconds later a drop of petrol splashed on the back of his outstretched hand. Quickly, he scrambled out. 'Hi! Biggles!' he called urgently. 'Come here!'

Biggles dropped his map and came at a run, followed more slowly by the others. 'What is it?' he asked anxiously.

'Petrol is leaking from somewhere.'

'Where?'

'It seems to be coming out of the main tank.'

Biggles said nothing. In a moment he was under the machine, feeling the fabric on the bottom of the fuselage. Almost as quickly he scrambled out, and swinging himself up to the cockpit, looked at the petrol gauge on the instrument-board. One glance was enough. Another second and he was down. 'Bear a hand, everybody,' he snapped. 'Get that fabric off – cut it if necessary.'

A few minutes of frantic effort and the truth was revealed. The rear main tank was leaking through a small round hole in the bottom. Biggles examined it closely before plugging it with a piece of chewing-gum from the small store they carried as a thirst preventative, and then covered it with a piece of adhesive plaster from the medicine chest.[1]

'That will have to do for the time being,' he said quietly. 'We can do nothing more. If we try siphoning what little petrol we have left into another tank we shall lose most of it by evaporation.'

Algy looked at him with startled eyes. 'How much is there left?' he asked in an odd tone of voice.

Biggles hesitated for a moment. 'About half as much as we should need to get back to the nearest point of civilization,' he answered, speaking very slowly and distinctly. 'You remember that before we started I insisted that we should

[1] More than one famous long-distance airman has mended a leaking tank or petrol-lead in this fashion.

carry enough fuel to get us back should anything go wrong
with the caravan.'

'Yes – we did that.'

'Quite. Well, as a result of this leak, I reckon we've enough
petrol left, including what is in the gravity tank, for a little
more than one hour's flying. We were flying over desert for
more than three hours getting here. Work that out for yourself.'

'We shall be all right when the caravan arrives,' declared
Ginger optimistically.

Biggles threw him a sidelong glance. 'Yes,' he said, 'we
shall – provided it *does* arrive.'

'If it doesn't?' asked Kadar.

Biggles smiled faintly. 'You should know better than anyone else the answer to that question. I think it would be better
not to dwell on that – anyway, not until tonight, by which
time the caravan should be here.'

'What an unfortunate accident,' muttered Kadar.

Biggles laughed harshly. 'Accident! That hole in our tank
could only have been made with one thing, a pointed instru-
ment; and, believe me, that couldn't happen by accident.'

CHAPTER 5

THE END OF THE TRAIL

THE caravan did not arrive that evening. It did not arrive that night. Nor did it arrive the next day, although just as the sun was sinking below the horizon, and the purple dusk was closing in around them, the airmen had their first glimpse of the primeval dwellers of the endless sands when a party of those mysterious, blue-veiled warriors of the desert, the dreaded Tuareg, the 'Forgotten God', came riding out of the sunset.

The airmen were sitting talking round their meagre stores on the edge of the oasis when Kadar suddenly stiffened and glanced up. 'Tuareg,' he said softly. 'Take no notice. They may mean no harm – or they may. One can never be sure.'

The others turned to look. From out of the west, looming gigantic in the half light, came a line of veiled warriors mounted on tall Mehari camels. They rode in silence, the feet of their mounts making no noise on the sand. Looking neither to right nor left, without showing by sign or movement that they had seen the hated *Roumi*, the white man – which they must have done – they passed on, as sinister, as evil, as impassive as death, their shrouded figures the embodiment of hostility and cold malevolence. Gazing straight ahead in the gathering darkness, like spectral shapes they disappeared behind a dune, leaving behind them a chill of sullen enmity.

Biggles drew a deep breath. 'It looks as if we shall have to take turns to keep guard,' he said.

But the night passed without the return of the warriors. When the dawn came they were out of sight.

The day passed, and another night; and when the following morning the long-overdue caravan was still unsighted, Biggles called a council of war, for all nerves were on edge with the anxiety of waiting.

'Well, everybody, this is the position,' he announced gravely, as they forgathered under a palm-tree near the idle machine. 'I think you all know how we are fixed, but I will just run over the situation so that there can be no misunderstanding. Our stores have not arrived. They were scheduled to be here three days ago. It is obvious, therefore, that something has gone wrong, and although it may sound pessimistic, my own feeling is that they will not now arrive at all. In the ordinary way, that need not have caused us anything worse than irritation that our plans should have miscarried, but the incident of the leaking tank has altered the position very considerably. As you know, I made allowance for the possible non-arrival of the caravan by carrying enough petrol to get us back home again independently of it. Of that spare petrol more than two-thirds has been lost in a manner which suggests foul play. The same influence might account for the non-arrival of the caravan – we do not know; but what it boils down to is this:

'In still air, we are three hours from Dakhel, and still more from Siwah, those being our nearest points of contact with the outside world. We have enough petrol for one hour's flying, so whichever way we go we shall be compelled to land more than two hundred miles from our objective. I need hardly say that such a course is utterly out of the question. It would be plain suicide. The alternative to that is, we stay here. Very well, what is the position then? We have left out of the emergency rations which we always carry three small tins of bully beef, a few biscuits, six cubes of Bovril, some chocolate, and one or two odds and ends. In short, we have enough food, used sparingly, to last for another two days. Two days, three days, or four days, it matters little; the end must be the same. Still, while we stay here we shall not die of thirst or starvation. There is water in the spring, which Kadar assures me has never been known to dry up, and there are dates on the palms. How long we can live on a diet of dates and water without going crazy, I do not know, but it is at least possible to live. Arabs exist on nothing more than that for weeks on end; whether we shall be able to remains to be seen.

'Now as far as I can see there is only one course open to us. We can't reach civilization, so we must, therefore, stay here; but before we resign ourselves to that it is possible for us to make a last attempt to get into touch with the outside world. As I have said, we still have a little petrol in the tank, enough for an hour's flying, possibly a little more, but a few minutes either way is neither here nor there. We might as well use that petrol while we have it, for in a hot dry temperature like this it will have evaporated inside a week. For desert use, petrol in cans has to be hermetically sealed; that which we bought in Cairo to go with the caravan was sealed in that way. On what petrol we have left our cruising speed gives us a range of about seventy-five miles; that is to say, we can fly seventy-five miles out and get back here. My suggestion is that we make a reconnaissance in the direction of Siwah, that being the direction from which the caravan should have come, in the hope of seeing something of it. If we find it, all so well and good; if we do not, then we must return here and resign ourselves to the inevitable. There is always a chance, of course, that, when we do not return, Kadar's father will send out a rescue party to look for us, but some time must elapse before that is likely to happen, because, as we declared our intention of being away for some weeks, we shall not be reported missing until the end of that time. Well, that's all. If anyone has a better suggestion, let him make it, but I can think of nothing else myself.'

Biggles took out one of his three remaining cigarettes, broke it in halves, gave Algy one half, and then lighted both with the same match.

'It isn't much use trying to think of an alternative plan, for the simple reason that there isn't one,' declared Algy. 'The one you have suggested is the only thing we can do.'

'I've nothing to add to that,' said Ginger.

Kadar shook his head. 'Nor I, except that I am sorry to have brought you —'

Biggles waved him to silence. 'Very well, then, that's settled,' he declared.

'When do you propose to make this trip?' asked Algy.

'Now. There is no point in waiting. From the top of the palm I climbed at dawn I estimated that I could see between thirty and forty miles. The caravan was not in sight. That means that even if it is approaching it will not get here before dark. By tomorrow morning we shall have lost, due to evaporation, perhaps five per cent of our petrol. That is why I say let us go now, and, if necessary, learn the worst at once.'

The wisdom of this plan was apparent to everyone, and preparations were at once made for the trip. Every available vessel that would hold water was filled and put aboard, as well as what was left of the stores and a quantity of dates. When there was nothing more to be done the dust-covers were removed and stowed away, and the airmen took their places.

Biggles walked the entire distance of the probable run before he attempted to take off, but the sand, while soft on the surface, was firm, and there were no obstacles. Satisfied that all was well, he climbed into the cockpit, and in a few moments the Tourer was in the air, climbing into the western sky.

As the machine gained altitude all eyes looked into the direction from which the caravan should come. The quivering needle of the altimeter crept round the dial until at length it rested on the ten-thousand mark, but as far as the eye could see not a moving speck broke the surface of the silent sea of sand.

Biggles turned to Algy, who was sitting next to him. His face was grim. 'Another five minutes and we must turn back,' he said.

Algy nodded, his eyes still questing the western horizon. A moment or two later he started. 'I can see something,' he said.

Biggles gazed long and steadily ahead. 'Yes, there is something,' he agreed, 'but it doesn't move.'

'No, it's nothing alive,' returned Algy.

Another two minutes went by and Biggles spoke again. His voice was hard and dry. 'It is a caravan,' he said. 'Or the remains of one,' he added, dropping his voice.

'The remains of one – I think.'

Biggles took the throttle in his left hand, and then hesitated, uncertain as to the wisest course when so much depended on the issue. 'What shall we do?' he asked Algy. 'I ought to turn in another minute. Dare we go down? We are eighty miles from home. I shall not be able to make up any altitude that I lose.'

Algy glanced up, caught Biggles's eyes, but looked away quickly. 'Go down,' he said. 'The petrol may still be there. If it isn't, we're sunk, anyway.'

Biggles was faced with a gamble in which life was at stake, and he knew it. Upon the events of the next few minutes hung all their lives. If the sand was soft and he attempted to land on it, it would be the end beyond all possible shadow of doubt. Even if they did not land, the flight back, with the fast-dwindling petrol, would be a nightmare. Already he doubted if they could reach the oasis, although they might get within walking distance.

The noise of the engines died away suddenly as he cut the throttle, and thereby announced his decision. The Tourer's nose tilted down and the machine began to lose height; and as it went down the details of the scene on the ground grew clearer. As Algy had prophesied, it was not a caravan. It was the remains of one. Soon it became possible to distinguish objects – camels lying outstretched on the sand – saddles – bundles – garments – bodies.

'There has been dirty work done here,' muttered Algy, white-faced.

'Tuareg work, I fancy,' answered Biggles through his teeth.

'What are you going to do?'

'I must land.'

'It's a ghastly risk.'

'I know. But I must go down. Some of those poor devils may be only wounded. Again, there is just a chance that there may be some petrol in those panniers. Either way, it is a risk that we have got to take.'

Algy nodded. 'Go ahead,' was all he said.

With the wind moaning over the wings, the aeroplane swept lower. Twice Biggles circled, unable to bring himself to take the terrible risk of landing. His eyes scrutinized the ground yard by yard. It was at least clear of obstacles. The third time he clenched his teeth and glided in to land. Beads of perspiration stood out on his face, so intense was the mental strain as he flattened out. The next few seconds would decide their fate. It was queer to think of that. Five seconds. The scene became unreal – was it really happening, or was he dreaming? The muscles of his face twitched as the wheels touched and the machine quivered, and he braced himself for the inevitable somersault should the sand be soft. The wheels touched again. There was a jar as the tail wheel dragged, and the next moment the machine was running sluggishly over the ground. The sand was soft, but not too soft, although it pulled the machine up quickly.

Algy did not wait for it quite to finish its run. He opened the door, jumped out, and ran towards the scene of the tragedy. A cloud of flies (for there are flies even in the desert) rose into the air as he dashed up; then he recoiled in horror. In his life he had seen some unpleasant sights, but that which now met his eyes nearly made him ill. Still, he ran to the nearest pannier, saw that it was empty, and hurried on to the next.

A moment or two later Biggles joined him. 'Petrol,' he said tersely. 'Is there any petrol?'

Algy looked up. His face was ashen and curiously set. 'No,' he said quietly. 'Not a drop.'

CHAPTER 6

THE *HABOOB*

Biggles waited for the others to come up. He turned to Kadar. 'This was our caravan, wasn't it?'

Unashamed tears were running down Kadar's face. 'Yes,' he answered chokingly. 'There is old Mahomout, the caravan leader. He has ridden his last trail. What can we do with them?'

'Nothing,' answered Biggles shortly. 'If anyone is alive we will take him back to the Oasis, although heaven knows what we can do for him there even if we do. You'd better leave it to me to find out, although from what I can see it will be a waste of time. Are these – mutilations – Tuareg work, Kadar?'

'Yes.'

'All right. Well, we are in no case to be squeamish. Go through the panniers and collect any food you can find, also any water-skins.' Biggles turned away to commence his gruesome task.

'It is as I thought,' he said in a hollow voice, when a few minutes later he joined the others again. 'They are all dead. I wonder why the camels all seem to be in such poor condition.'

'The others will have been taken,' replied Kadar.

'They would be needed to carry the petrol,' put in Algy.

Biggles knitted his brow. 'These shocking murders may

60

have been Tuareg work,' he muttered, 'but why should they
burden themselves with petrol? What use could it be to them?
My feeling is that although Tuaregs may have done the work,
there was somebody else behind them. Either that, or they
had definite orders to take the petrol. Look, that is the way
they went.' He pointed to where a broad trail of hoof-marks
wound away into the dunes. 'The murderers went that way, so
the Arabs we saw at the oasis could not have been respons-
ible – that is, unless they made a detour. But we mustn't
stand talking here. The sooner we get back to the oasis the
better. My heavens! Isn't the heat dreadful? Did you find any
food?'

Possibly on account of the tragedy, the lesser demon of
heat had been temporarily overlooked, but they now began
to be conscious of it.

Algy pointed to a little heap of tins. 'Those were all in the
same pannier,' he said. 'I found it under one of the dead
camels, which is probably why it was overlooked. There are
a few tins of meat and some dried fruits.'

'We'll take them with us,' declared Biggles. 'I fancy we
shall need them. Come on, let's get back. We can do nothing
more here.'

They all helped to carry the salvage into the machine. As
they approached it Biggles pointed to the wheels; already the
tyres had half disappeared into the sand.

'She's sinking. An hour, and we should not be able to
budge her,' he said. 'We shall have to watch out for that sort
of thing.'

A last glance at the pitiable spectacle behind them and they
took their places. The port engine roared as Biggles swung
round to get into position to take off over the same ground
on which he had landed. Reaching the place, he closed his
eyes for a moment before choosing a mark on which to fly,
for the dunes appeared to be rocking in the heat. Then,

slowly, he opened the throttle. The machine surged forward, running more and more lightly as it gathered speed. It took a long run to get off, but in the end the wheels unstuck, and at a height of a few hundred feet Biggles gave a sigh of relief and turned its nose to the east.

He allowed the machine to climb up to a thousand feet, then he levelled out and throttled back to the most economical cruising speed, all the while holding the machine as steady as he could in the choppy atmosphere. The 'bumps' were almost continuous, and often so severe that it was necessary for the airmen to hold themselves in their places by gripping their seats.

For perhaps five minutes these conditions prevailed, and then, without warning, the Tourer was impelled upwards to more than double its altitude by one of the most vicious 'bumps' Biggles had ever experienced. The effect was almost precisely that of going up in an express lift; but whereas a lift is seldom more than a hundred feet high, the bump in question was sustained for more than a thousand. Kadar clasped his stomach and rolled his eyes. 'I shall be sick if it does that again,' he said desperately.

Hardly were the words out of his mouth when the machine dropped several hundred feet like a stone, as if all support had been snatched from under its wings – as indeed it had. At the bottom of the bump it struck solid air again with a shock that made it quiver.

'Getting rocky,' murmured Biggles laconically to Algy, without any particular concern, for he had flown through bumps too often to be alarmed by them, and knew that in a reliable aircraft, with no risk of structural failure, there was no danger.

As he levelled out at the bottom of the bump something made him glance to the left, which, as he was flying eastward, was towards the north. For perhaps five seconds he stared unbelievingly, then he turned to Algy with an air of almost hopeless resignation.

'I don't usually give up,' he said, 'but this looks like settling any further argument as far as we are concerned.'

Algy, staring towards the northern horizon, saw a terrifying spectacle. Racing towards them, blotting out the blue sky as effectively as a thick curtain, was what appeared to be an enormous brown cloud that twisted and writhed within itself as it bore down on them. He knew what it was as well as Biggles.

'It's a *haboob*,'[1] he said calmly. 'What are you going to do about it?'

In normal circumstances only one course is open to a pilot who encounters one of these terrifying meteorological disturbances. He must go down quickly, land, turn the nose of his machine into the wind, and anchor it by tying sand-bags to the wings, tail, and fuselage, after which he takes refuge in or under the machine. The bags are carried empty, of course, but they are soon filled with the most common commodity in the desert. Aeroplanes of the French Air Force, and passenger machines operating in North Africa, are nearly always provided with bags for this purpose. But they adhere to regular routes, where they are soon found if for any reason the machine is unable to take off again after the storm has passed.

Biggles's position was a very different one. Should he follow the usual practice and land, there was no hope of rescue in the event of his machine being damaged, as it was not unlikely to be. He was well aware of the danger of trying to get above a *haboob*, against which pilots are warned, even if his tanks had been full. Yet what else could he do? He could not hope to reach the oasis before the swirling sand

---

[1] *Haboob*. A severe sand-storm, far worse than the more common dust-storm; it may extend from the ground to a height of 10,000 feet.

engulfed him, and to run before the storm would, within half an hour, see him on the ground with empty tanks in the very worst part of the desert, perhaps the most inaccessible spot in the world, in the path of the sand demon. In the short time he had for reflection it seemed to him that his only possible hope – how slim it was he knew only too well – lay in getting above the sand, still keeping on his course, trusting either that he would get beyond the disturbed area, which seemed unlikely as he could not see the eastern extremity of it, or that the *haboob* would soon pass. With these forlorn hopes in view he shoved the throttle wide open and began to climb as steeply as his engines would take him.

He managed to reach six thousand feet before the first sharp spatter of sand struck the side of the machine. The sun had become a fast-fading orange ball. He could still see the ground dimly, as through a thick brown haze, but, even as he watched, it was blotted out, and the Tourer was alone in the heart of the storm. For a time visibility was limited to a sort of dim twilight, but as he continued to climb, listening to every beat of the engines for the first warning of seizure, it became somewhat lighter. With the needle of his altimeter registering twelve thousand feet he was almost clear, with the sky showing as a greenish ceiling; but it was on his petrol gauge that his eyes were fixed. He was still running on his main tank, but it was nearly down to zero, and he knew that at any moment the petrol supply might fail.

He had no idea of where he was because he did not know the speed of the wind that was blowing at right angles across his path of flight. He knew the compass-bearing of the oasis, but without knowing his speed of drift he could only hold his course by guesswork. He estimated the speed of the wind at fifty to sixty miles an hour, but in view of what subsequently happened it must have been considerably more than that during the worst of the storm. The ground was buried under a ten-thousand-feet-thick layer of flying sand, so what lay beneath that he did not know, although he could only assume – and hope – that it was the desert over which he had flown on the outward journey.

He had now throttled back again to the minimum speed that would keep the machine airborne, for his chief concern was to conserve his petrol in order to remain in the air as long as possible. It may have been in some measure due to this that nearly another ten minutes elapsed before a warning cough from one of his engines told him that his main tank was nearly dry. He held on until the engines began choking, and then switched over to the gravity tank, which contained, at the outside limit, enough petrol to keep them in the air for another ten minutes. A fine film of dust had settled on his lips, and he wiped them with his sleeve before turning to speak to Algy.

'I should say that we shall be extremely fortunate if we hit the ground within sight of the oasis,' he said quietly. 'If we do, I am afraid it will be more by luck than judgement. I wouldn't swear to our position to within fifty miles. The wind speed up here might be anything – anything up to a hundred miles an hour. I don't know, and it would be a clever man who could guess. I don't fancy going down into the pea-soup underneath us, but we shall have to in a minute or two.'

'Well, at least we shan't hit somebody's wireless-mast or chimney-pot,' asserted Algy optimistically.

'I only wish there was a risk of that, believe me,' murmured Biggles. 'Better tell the boys inside to be ready to jump clear when we hit. I won't guarantee to put her down the right side up in this infernal murk.'

Algy did as he was requested, and as he returned, the engines, after a choking splutter, cut out dead. The propellers stopped. The roar died away, to be replaced by the not-unmusical murmur of wind in the wires. Biggles pushed the joystick forward. The nose went down, and almost at once the brown twilight began to close in around them again. He did not speak. The situation did not call for comment. He, Algy, and Ginger knew precisely what was happening, and what was likely to happen. They were flying blind. Presently they would reach the ground, and the violence of the impact depended on whether or not Biggles saw it. The needle of the altimeter began to creep back, 8,000 – 7,000 – 6,000.

Algy coughed, the noise seeming to be curiously loud.

The machine continued to lose height, with Biggles's eyes alternating between the false horizon on the instrument-board and the altimeter. There was no need for him to look at the speed indicator, for he could judge his approximate speed by the feel of the joystick.

They were down to a thousand feet, and Algy began looking over the side. There was still no sign of the ground, and he said so, jerking his head back sharply as a great black bulk appeared to float past them.

'What the dickens was that?' he cried sharply.

Biggles raised his eyes for an instant. 'If I didn't know better I should say it was a mountain.'

'It was!' yelled Algy suddenly. 'Look out!'

'Impossible!' snapped Biggles, and then flung the joystick over as a great sombre mass loomed suddenly in front. The machine went over on its side, but he righted it again instantly. With every nerve in his body strained to breaking-point, he swerved again as a jagged peak leapt up out of the gloom and appeared to clutch at the machine. He flashed a glance at the altimeter. As inexorable as fate the needle was creeping back – 400 – 300. His eyes switched to the darkness ahead, and then to the vague shadows underneath.

'Look out!' yelled Algy again. 'I can see the carpet.'

So could Biggles. Or he saw something, he was not sure what it was. He snatched the stick back, felt the machine falter, and waited for the stall. The crest of a solitary palm floated past his side window, then a cairn of stones. He flattened out and braced himself for the crash. *Bump!* He felt the wheels strike something solid, and knew that he had bounced. *Bang!* Again the wheels struck, and the machine reared like a bucking horse. Another brief interval, seeming like an eternity in the pent-up anxiety of the moment, and the wheels struck again. This time they held the ground, although the machine lurched sickeningly. Then came a series of minor jars, another slight bounce, and the machine ran to a standstill.

There was a moment of utter silence, almost frightening in its suddenness. Then Algy spoke.

'Well, we are at least on the ground,' he said simply. 'And that's something.'

Biggles smiled wearily. 'It's a lot,' he said as he leaned back, and Algy noticed that his face was strangely drawn.

CHAPTER 7

LOST IN THE DESERT

'WELL, I suppose we might as well get out and see where we've arrived at,' announced Ginger.

'I fancy we shall be lucky to do that,' answered Biggles. 'In any case, we had better sit where we are until the sand settles a bit, or we shall be choked. The storm has passed, but it has left all this stuff in the air, so we had better wait for it to thin a bit.'

'Pass me a drop of water, somebody,' requested Algy.

'Go steady with it,' warned Biggles. 'We don't know where any more is coming from.'

They bore the stifling heat inside the cabin for another half hour, and then, the sand having thinned considerably, they got out and looked about them. Biggles pointed to the machine, coated with a thick layer of sand, so that the fabric resembled nothing so much as sandpaper.

'What a pretty problem that will be for some explorer in a few hundreds of years' time, wondering how an aeroplane got here,' he observed. 'He will probably pack it up and take it home and have it put under a glass case in a museum, in the same way as we should a chariot.' While Biggles had been speaking he had been looking round. 'I may be mistaken, and I hope I am, but this place doesn't strike me as being what you might call a health resort,' he concluded.

'You're right, it doesn't,' agreed Algy.

Nevertheless, they were able to judge how lucky they had been in getting down without a serious accident, for the place in which the machine had landed was a narrow *wadi*, or valley, between forbidding outcrops of rock. All around them towered gaunt, barren hills, their peaks still half obscured in a mist of sand. Rocks lay all about them. There was little else, except the floor of the *wadi*, which was a long expanse of sand that had silted in – the accumulation of years. There was no sign of life, but one or two stunted palms, their fronds brown and withered, suggested that there might be water deep down in the earth; but as there was not a blade of grass, green or otherwise, there was clearly none near the surface.

'Gosh! What a sun-smitten dustbin,' muttered Ginger disgustedly. 'I wonder what lies beyond the edge of the *wadi*. I have a feeling that there ought to be an oasis not far away.'

'And I have a feeling that if there is we shall have found what we were looking for,' returned Biggles dryly.

The others stared at him.

'You mean – the Lost Oasis?' cried Ginger.

'Why not?' continued Biggles. 'We were flying due east when the *haboob* caught us. It came from the north, therefore our line of flight must have been something south of east – say due south-east. Speaking from memory, according to my map no oasis occurs in that direction for hundreds of miles. Nor, for that matter, are there any mountains shown. If there is an oasis here it is certainly an unknown one, even if it is not the legendary Lost Oasis of – what was the name of it? – Zenzura.'

'By the head of my father, I believe you are right!' cried Kadar. 'We have found by accident what we came to look for.'

Biggles nodded. 'Well, Kadar,' he said, 'if it is, I hope you are satisfied with your find; but you'll pardon me, I hope, if I do not go into ecstasies about it. The thing that exercises my mind at the moment is not how to find the Lost Oasis, or what to do with it if we have indeed found it, but how we are going to get home again.'

'But suppose this *is* the Lost Oasis?' cried Kadar enthusiastically.

Biggles regarded him moodily. 'Suppose it is? What are you going to do with it, anyway? It's all yours as far as I'm concerned. Personally, I'd swap the lot for a tuft of nice green grass or even a bunch of stinging-nettles.'

'It is rather depressing, I must confess,' admitted Kadar, somewhat abashed.

'Depressing!' Biggles laughed harshly. 'I could find a better word than that for it.'

'I think the first thing to do is to try to ascertain if it *is* the Lost Oasis,' declared Kadar.

Biggles eyed him sadly. 'You do, do you?'

'Yes; I fancy I saw a cairn of stones farther back —'

'Listen, laddie,' interrupted Biggles. 'From what I can see of it, you are going to have plenty of time to trot about looking for heaps of stones. What we need is a nice heap of *scones*. We are not likely to get very fat on a diet of boulders, so before we start sharpening our teeth on the crusty crags of your precious oasis, let us try to find something softer. Haven't you realized yet that if we don't find water within twenty-four hours, when the sand clears and the sun comes out, we shall be frizzled like kippers on a grill? It seems to me that the sooner we start looking for something to drink and eat, the better.'

'Yes,' agreed Kadar. 'Of course. I am sorry. I was carried away by my excitement.'

'Well, calm yourself, and try to think of something to carry us away from this oven,' Biggles told him. 'That should give you something to ponder on. Well, come on, let's start exploring.'

'All of us?' asked Ginger.

Biggles thought for a moment. 'No, I don't think we'd better all go, in case a bunch of stray Tuareg drift in and steal what little food we've got. We don't want to carry it about with us, so someone had better stay here and look after things. You stay, Algy. I'll go and have a look round. Ginger can come with me; and I'd better take Kadar in case we meet anyone – not that I think it's likely – because he can speak the local languages.'

'Will you take the rifle?' asked Algy. With the exception of their pistols, a rifle was the only weapon they had brought with them. They had tried to avoid unnecessary weight, but a rifle had been brought for emergencies, although Kadar had stated that it was most unlikely that it would be needed.

'No, I will leave it here with you,' replied Biggles. 'We shan't go far. We ought to be able to see quite a long way from the top of the next hill.' So saying, he slung a water-bottle over his shoulder, adjusted a pair of the dark glasses with which the expedition had been equipped, without which blindness soon comes in the desert, and set off down the *wadi* with Ginger and Kadar on either side of him. They, also, wore sun-glasses.

The heat was intense. The sand that had been whirled high into the air by the *haboob* had either settled again or been drawn on by the vortex, and the sun, now immediately over-head, probed the bare, tortured earth with bars of white heat. There was no escape, for there was no shade. The rocks quivered as they flung back the heat they could not absorb, and the sandy floor of the *wadi* became a gleaming carpet that scorched the explorers' feet through the thick rope soles of their desert shoes.

Before they had reached the end of the *wadi* the sky had entirely cleared, and the depression had become a cauldron. The white glare had given way to yellow haze, distorting the rocks into fantastic shapes, and making it impossible to judge distance. The hill at the end of the *wadi* appeared to recede as they went forward, but they reached it at last, and climbed it, only to find that their view was interrupted by a slightly higher hill in front of it.

'This is awful,' muttered Ginger, who was beginning to feel the first symptoms of the dreadful desert lassitude. He felt his face curiously, wondering why he did not perspire, not realizing that the fiery heat of the desert dries all moisture as fast as it exudes through the skin.

Biggles said nothing. He went on, with gnawing anxiety in his heart. He knew that his casual remark about the necessity for finding water was literally true. If they did not find it in the next few hours, while they had the strength to search for it, they would perish.

They climbed the next hill, and Biggles's heart sank as he saw a great face of cliff in front of him, obstructing what lay beyond and forming an insurmountable obstacle. Biting his lip with vexation and disappointment, he faced to either side in turn. It was the same everywhere. Rock and sand. Nothing more. To the left of the hill, however, the ground fell away sharply into a deep gully, and towards this he turned his steps.

'You know more about this sort of thing than we do, Kadar,' he said, 'but I imagine that we should stand a better chance of finding water on the lower ground.'

'Yes, although it will be hotter.'

They went on, traversed the gully, only to find that it led into a yet deeper one. And all around was the ghastly sameness of rock and sand.

Biggles stopped. 'This is no use,' he said simply. 'We had better not go any farther without a bigger water supply, or without Algy. We've come some distance already. Let us get back and suspend operations until the sun goes down. It will be cooler after dark, and we shall be able to find our way in the moonlight.'

They went back through the gully, climbed the hill, and descended the other side, retracing their footsteps – as they thought. Suddenly Biggles stopped again. 'This isn't the hill we came up,' he said in a hard voice.

'It must be. I think we are only going down a different way,' muttered Ginger, but his voice lacked conviction.

They went on down to the bottom, where Biggles again stopped. He pointed to a huge, mushroom-shaped rock, the base of which had been worn to a mere stalk by countless centuries of erosion. 'We didn't come past that,' he said.

'I think the *wadi* is here,' suggested Kadar, in a voice that had become strangely hoarse.

Again they went forward, hurrying now, to the great cleft in the rocks which Kadar had indicated. But as they reached it they pulled up short, staring aghast at an inferno of rocks and sand which they had certainly not seen before.

Biggles passed his hand wearily over his face. He no longer attempted to deceive himself. 'We're lost,' he said simply.

'Yes, we're lost.' Kadar sat down and buried his face in his arms. 'It was my fault,' he went on miserably. 'I should have known better. The Tuareg have a saying which is taught to their children as soon as they are old enough to understand. It means, "Never leave the trail".'

'But it seems impossible that we could lose ourselves so quickly,' said Ginger.

Kadar shook his head. 'In the desert one can become hopelessly lost, and die of thirst, within a mile of camp. It has happened many times.'

'Well, there is only one thing left. Perhaps Algy will hear this.' Biggles took out his pistol, and, pointing the muzzle into the air, fired three shots at regular intervals.

If there was a reply they did not hear it. All they heard were the echoes of the shots reverberating from hill to hill until they died away in the distance. A piece of rock detached itself from a nearby cliff and fell with an astonishing amount of noise for its size. After that there was silence. Dead, utter silence. Not merely the lesser noise of civilized countries; it was a complete absence of sound.

Ginger felt a thrill of fear, nearly approaching panic. A cold hand seemed to clutch his heart. He realized that he was very thirsty, and also very tired.

'We should never have left our water-supply,' muttered Kadar.

'It isn't much use saying now what we should or should not have done,' returned Biggles bitterly. 'The question is, what are we going to do?'

The others did not answer.

'Well, it isn't much use standing here,' continued Biggles, striking at a fly that persisted in settling on his face. 'Confound these flies. Where the dickens do they come from, anyway?'

'Wherever you go in Egypt you will find "Gippy" flies,' answered Kadar wearily, as he stood up. 'Let us go back to that deep gully and see where it leads. The ground sloped downwards there, and the bottom of the depression is the most likely place to find water.'

They dragged their weary legs back up the hill, and down the other side, but there was no sign of the gully they sought.

Biggles laughed harshly, an unpleasant sound without any humour in it. 'This place is bewitched,' he muttered viciously.

'Of course it is,' returned Kadar quietly. 'Now you know why the Tuareg call this district the Region of Devils. It is full of evil spirits. It is the *djinns* who send the *haboobs*.'

Biggles unslung his water-bottle. 'There is no need for us to die of thirst before we must,' he said casually. 'A mouthful each – no more.'

The water was quite warm, and did little to slake their raging thirst, but Biggles recorked the bottle carefully. After that they went on.

They did not go in any particular direction. One way was the same as another. More and more flies appeared, until they hung in a black cloud over their heads, and although they struck at them repeatedly, they settled on eyes, nostrils, and even crawled into their ears. Once Ginger in a fury turned and slashed at them with his helmet, but it made no difference, and he stumbled on, panting.

The afternoon wore on, with the sun, a searing ball of fire, sinking all too slowly in the west. They had not the remotest idea of where they were, or even if they were walking round and round in the same area. It was all alike. Rock and sand. Never was there the slightest promise of the water they sought.

Late in the afternoon they thought they had come to a ruined town, and they ran forward eagerly, thinking that it could not have existed there without a water-supply. But it was only rocks, hundreds of tall, mushroom-shaped rocks, like a forest of gigantic toadstools; and more and more did Ginger appreciate the Tuareg description of the Region of Devils.

The heat in this petrified forest of fungi – as Biggles called it – was awful, but they stumbled on, wetting their lips at more and more frequent intervals from the fast-dwindling water-supply. It was that or madness. Already Ginger was walking through a dim yellow world in which ghostly figures marched beside him. Once he pulled up dead, convinced that in some mysterious way a line of camels had suddenly appeared; but they were only rocks, and he stumbled on, walking automatically. Presently flecks of vivid blue began to dance before his eyes. They merged until they became a quivering line, and he gave a shout, thinking that it was sunlight playing on water.

Biggles turned sharply. 'What's the matter?'

'Can you see anything ahead?' mumbled Ginger.

'No,' answered Biggles shortly. Then he laughed, a horrid cackling sound. 'Only rocks,' he said. 'Rocks and sand.'

Ginger reeled on, knowing that he had been mistaken. He knew, too, that he was near the end of his endurance. Biggles realized it, and passed him the water-bottle.

Ginger shook it, and by the sound knew that it was nearly empty. He handed it back.

'Drink it,' ordered Biggles. 'If you fall out we shall have to stay with you.'

Ginger allowed the precious drops – barely a mouthful – to trickle through his black, parched lips. He threw the bottle away.

Biggles picked it up and went on.

The sun sank behind the hills; at once the heat diminished and the relief brought a temporary respite. They came to a cliff. There seemed to be no way through it, and Biggles was about to turn when he saw a cave, a mere crack in the rock. 'Let's rest in there for a minute or two,' he suggested. 'It will be cooler.'

As they reached the fissure Kadar stopped suddenly, staring at the piled-up sand at the entrance. His eyes opened wide and an extraordinary expression crept over his face. He closed his eyes for a moment, shook his head, and then stared again. With a quivering forefinger he pointed at the sand.

The others, leaning forward to look, saw a number of imprints on the sand such as a large bird might make, and while their weary brains were still trying to grasp the significance of the tracks Kadar uttered a hoarse cry and rushed into the fissure. Understanding at last, they followed. Just inside was an unbelievable pool of pale-green water.

In a moment they had all flung themselves down and buried their faces in the cool liquid.

CHAPTER 8

THE TOMBS OF THE DEAD

AFTER Ginger had drunk to repletion he smiled wanly and, looking about him, noted with some surprise that the silent pool was not, as he had imagined, a new discovery of their own. All around the edges of the limpid water lay signs of man's intrusion, although there was no means of knowing whether they had been there for a month, a year, a century, or even more. Date-stones, a few gnawed bones, pieces of broken ostrich-shells, and a shattered spear-haft lay on the smooth hard sand, while in a corner – a gruesome sight – against the rock wall, in a semi-reclining position, reposed a skeleton.

'That's better,' observed Biggles, sitting back. 'We found this place just about in time. Queer sort of place to find water, isn't it, Kadar?'

'No. In the desert you sometimes find water in the most surprising places. This sort of formation is not uncommon. These pools are known to all who dwell in the desert, and have been known for countless generations. This one may have been here for thousands of years.'

'But where does the water come from?' asked Ginger.

'Condensation on the hill above at certain times of the year. The moisture condenses on the rock, collects in pockets and cavities, and seeps down through the heart of the mountain – which is why it is so cool – until it arrives in an impervious basin such as this, where, since it can get no farther, it must stay.'

Nothing more was said for a minute or two. The weary travellers were content to rest in the refreshing shade. The dim, unearthly green light that diffused the fissure was a pleasant change after the glare outside. Soliloquizing, Biggles realized that men had probably rested there in the same way for countless generations, perhaps since the birth of time. At last, seeing that the dusk was gathering in the gully, he rose to his feet.

'We must try to get back to Algy,' he said, 'although how that is to be done is more than I can imagine. Having found water, and knowing what it is like to be without it, I am loath to leave it, but we cannot exist on water alone. We need food. Still, we have learned our lesson. When we leave here we will blaze a trail, either in the sand, or by marking the rocks, so that we can find our way back again.'

'I think it would be better to wait here for a little while longer,' suggested Kadar. 'We shall travel more easily by moonlight.'

'I think you're right,' admitted Biggles.

So they sat down again and waited until the moon was flooding the gully with its cool light; then they moved towards the entrance. Reaching it, Biggles was about to step forward when he hesitated, peering at the ground a short distance beyond the mouth of the cave. Then he took a pace outside and looked up.

'That's funny,' he murmured, half to himself. 'What is causing that shadow to move?'

'What shadow?' asked Ginger.

'That one.' Biggles pointed to a wide area, reaching for some distance back, where the ground was darker than elsewhere. A stain seemed to be converging slowly on the fissure, and as they stood staring a slight sound became audible. It was a faint rustling, like the autumn wind among dead leaves.

'What the dickens is it?' asked Biggles again in a perplexed voice, and with just a hint of alarm. 'It seems to be alive.' His voice trailed away.

Kadar stepped forward, peering at the edge of the moving shadow. Suddenly, as if he had been thrust violently, he stumbled backward.

'They are scorpions!' His voice was hoarse with unutterable horror and loathing.

'Scorpions!' Biggles echoed the word incredulously.

'Yes. Thousands of them. Millions of them. I didn't know that scorpions drank water, but that must be why they are coming here – unless it is for us.'

'Good heavens! Let's get out of this!' cried Ginger, his voice rising to a high crescendo.

'Yes, but where can we go?' asked Biggles desperately. 'We can't get through that lot. One scorpion sting is bad enough, without —' He dashed out and looked up the face of the cliff.

'There's no escape that way,' he muttered, hurrying back to the others at the entrance to the cave.

For a moment they stared at the slowly approaching shadow of death – for a single scorpion sting can be fatal – the leading edge of which was now not more than half a dozen paces away. Unnoticed, a few of the poisonous creatures were in advance of the rest, and Biggles jumped aside only just in time to prevent one from climbing on to his shoe. He brought his heel down viciously on the crawling horror. 'No, you don't, you brute,' he muttered, and backed away hurriedly to the rear of the cave, where he struck a match from the box which he carried in his pocket. 'Thank goodness!' he said in tones of heartfelt relief. 'There's a way through here; we'd better see how far it goes.'

The others had joined him, and now stood staring rather apprehensively at a narrow black aperture in the farthest recess of the fissure.

'Don't for heaven's sake let us get lost in here. That would be worse than being lost outside,' said Ginger anxiously.

'I'd rather be lost than eaten – anyway, by scorpions,' declared Biggles. 'I'm not staying here.' He took his notebook from his pocket, and tearing out several leaves, rolled them into the form of spills. Lighting one of them with a match, he started off along the cave with the others following close behind.

He had not gone very far when the spill was knocked out of his hand, being, of course, extinguished. But before it went out he had a fleeting impression of a dark shape bearing down on it.

'What the deuce was that?' he cried, fumbling hastily for another match. In the momentary silence that followed his words a curious, leathery, fluttering sound could be heard; it was not unlike running water in the distance.

'Bats!' said Kadar.

At that moment something hit Ginger a hard blow in the face; instinctively he struck at it, but only succeeded in barking his knuckles against the wall of the cave.

Another match flared up, disclosing a host of dim shapes passing in a steady stream down the natural corridor over their heads towards the exit. One detached itself from the rest and made a dart at the match, but Biggles was ready, and he dashed it violently against the wall with a lightning sweep of his hand. It hit the rock with a thud and fell to the ground, where it lay fluttering. An unpleasant fetid smell became noticeable, but no one commented on it.

Biggles lighted another spill and went on. 'While there's only a single corridor we can't very well lose our way, at all events,' he exclaimed hopefully. 'There may be another way out somewhere. Let's keep going. Never mind these stinking bats. First, scorpions, now bats – my word! The Tuareg knew what they were talking about when they named this place the Region of Devils.'

The sandy floor now began to rise under their feet, but they went on, sometimes striking at the bats when they came too close to be comfortable, and keeping a good look out on either side for turnings. In this way they travelled for a considerable distance, and then, with surprising suddenness, the bats all disappeared. Kadar ventured an opinion – that was probably right – that as bats feed at night they had all gone out. Anyway, they had certainly disappeared, and presently Biggles called a halt.

'I don't think we need fear the scorpions any longer,' he said, 'so the only point in going farther seems to be the hope of finding another exit – not that we shall need one if the scorpions are considerate enough to retire to wherever they came from when it gets light. By the way, we had better be careful about picking up stones, or we may get stung; if I remember rightly, that is where they like to sit. There is one thing about going on, though: as it is dark outside we might pass an exit without seeing it, so it would perhaps be a better plan to stay where we are until it gets light.'

Everyone was tired, but nobody felt particularly like resting. They did, in fact, sit down on the sand for a time, but they soon found that in their precarious condition sleep was out of the question, so they abandoned all thought of it.

'We've been going uphill ever since we left the pool,' observed Biggles thoughtfully, 'so if we do happen to strike an opening it should be on fairly high ground, from where we ought to get a view of the surrounding country. We might possibly be high enough to spot the machine. Poor old Algy will be in a state by this time, I expect, but we can't do anything about it.'

After that another silence fell, in which Biggles passed the time usefully by folding a bunch of spills, using nearly all the pages of his notebook for the purpose. Several matches still remained in his box, and as Ginger had a petrol-lighter, there seemed to be no reason why they should run out of illumination.

'We've been to some queer places in our time, but I doubt if we ever passed a night in a stranger place than this – the middle of a mountain in an unexplored desert,' said Ginger, after a long interval.

'It will be a long time, I hope, before I pass another night in it, anyway,' replied Biggles. 'This silence gives me the jitters; it's like being in a tomb.'

Ginger shivered. 'That's a cheerful remark to make, I must say,' he returned indignantly. 'You're too near the mark to be pleasant, and I shall feel happier when I'm out of it. I'm ready to push on a bit farther if everyone else is.'

Everyone appeared to be more than willing, so they stood up and prepared to move on. Biggles struck a match, lighted a spill, and they started off, but they had not travelled very far when Biggles, who was leading, gave a sharp exclamation.

'There's something ahead,' he said. 'I can't quite make out what it is, but the cave seems to open out considerably into a sort of hall.'

A few more paces revealed that that was indeed the case, and they all stopped, staring about them in wonderment, not that they could see very much in the dim light of the flare. All they could perceive was that they were in a lofty chamber, almost like a church, the extremities of which were lost in gloom. Biggles took several new spills, opened them fanwise between his fingers, lighted them from the one already alight, and held them aloft. His eyes first went to the ceiling; then they travelled slowly down the walls.

'For a natural formation, this place seems to be extraordinarily free from stalactites and things,' he murmured. 'What the —'

There was a short silence in which they all stared at the lower part of the walls, which appeared to be hollowed out in the form of a honeycomb. In other words, they seemed to consist of a great number of small cavities, or compartments. And that was not all. There was something in each compartment.

Kadar solved the problem. 'You said just now that this place was like a tomb,' he said, instinctively dropping his voice to a whisper. 'That's exactly what it is. I have seen a place something like this before. We are in the tombs of the dead.'

Ginger experienced that unpleasant creepy feeling at the top of the spine sometimes described as the hair standing on end. 'Crumbs!' he muttered in a thin voice. 'Let's hop it.'

Biggles lighted some more spills to replace those that were nearly exhausted. 'That looks like one of the bodies fallen out,' he said, pointing to a huddled form on the floor. 'Perhaps the poor blighter was buried alive.'

Kadar, his archaeological instinct aroused, stepped eagerly towards it, but he had not taken more than two or three steps when, to the consternation of everybody, the figure suddenly sat bolt upright. The skin over its eyes rolled back, exposing the whites, and for a fleeting instant the yellow light of the flares played on a wrinkled, leathery face, a hairless head, and a thin, scraggy neck. Then, with a wild screech, the figure leapt to its feet and bounded across the floor. What became of it no one saw, for at the screech Ginger had let out a yell of horror; Kadar leapt back as though shot out of a catapult, and coming into violent contact with Biggles knocked him over, with the result that the place was plunged into darkness.

To Ginger it was a moment of supreme horror, a ghastly

nightmare from which he could not awake. He could hear Biggles muttering as he groped for his matches, but the sound was almost drowned by a terrified whimpering sound which he presently identified as coming from Kadar. Then a match flared up, revealing Biggles just scrambling to his feet, and Kadar with his arms folded over his face.

'Come on, let's get out of this perishing place,' muttered Biggles. 'I don't believe in spooks, but if this place isn't haunted I'll eat my helmet.'

The others picked themselves up, and, while they stood collecting their scattered wits, the silence was again broken, this time by a peculiar whispering sound that seemed to come from the far end of the chamber. Hardly had it died away when there was a queer swishing noise that increased rapidly in volume, and, a moment later, from the narrow cave from which the airmen had emerged burst a black torrent of bats.

For a moment Biggles stared at them uncomprehendingly, never dreaming of danger from that direction; but as one deliberately swooped at him, and another attached itself to the side of his face with its teeth and claws, he understood. He tore the repulsive creature from his face and hurled it to the ground; then, turning, he raced for the far end of the hall, shouting to the others to follow him.

They needed no second invitation, and they all bolted incontinently, to discover that the chamber diminished rapidly to a small tunnel, at the entrance of which they arrived just in time to see the mummified figure bounding along it on all fours.

'Keep going!' yelled Biggles, and, whirling round, fired two shots from his pistol into the thick of the bats that were following them. Then, lighting matches as he went, he hurried after the others, who were stumbling along by the feeble light of Ginger's petrol-lighter.

The noise made by the bats as they poured into the tunnel

was incredible, and certainly alarming, and Biggles was wondering feverishly what he could do to stem the attack when a narrow slit of crimson light appeared ahead. For a second he could not imagine what it could be, but then he realized with joy that it was the dawn, and that the passage must end there. Which, in fact, it did, and the fugitives dashed out at a speed that nearly cost them their lives; for the passage terminated in the side of the hill, which, while not exactly a precipice, was too steep for safe negotiation at the pace they were travelling.

Kadar, who was in front, saw the danger first and let out a warning cry, and in a moment they were all slipping and sliding on the hill-side, grabbing wildly at anything their clutching fingers could find to check their precipitate descent. With bruised hands and torn finger-nails, they finally managed to pull themselves up, only to sit and stare in amazement at the sight that met their eyes.

'The Tuareg are right,' announced Biggles with absolute conviction. 'This is, without doubt, the Kingdom of Devils.'

CHAPTER 9

THE HORROR IN THE POOL

THE bats did not pursue the airmen once they were in the open. For a minute or two they hung over the mouth of the cave like a dense black cloud, making a curious twittering noise; then, as suddenly as they had appeared, they streamed back into the cave as if they were being drawn by an invisible vortex, leaving the invaders of their domain to survey the scene that lay spread out before them. This they did without speaking.

The hill on which they were seated was one of several that sloped down to a central plain, in the manner of a basin. There was nothing unusual about these hills; indeed, they were of a monotonous uniformity, consisting entirely of rock which had been burnt by the sun to a pale, slaty grey, and worn by erosion into the most fantastic shapes. It was no doubt due entirely to the natural circular watershed thus formed that the centre of this depression was in startling contrast to the rest. It was, briefly, an oasis, and, judging by the verdancy of the palms and other foliage, one of particular fertility. In places the palms had been cleared, leaving open spaces in which flourished what appeared to be corn.

From the centre of this refreshing prospect rose an impressive, dome-shaped hill, clothed for about half its height with palms and giant cacti; but then, due possibly to the failure of the essential water, they thinned out quickly, leaving the top of the dome bare of vegetation, so that the village which surmounted it stood out in high relief.

'Village' is, perhaps, a misleading word, for it was at once clear that most of the buildings were in ruins. For the rest, it consisted of a solid bank of dwellings set in the form of terraces, bleached grey by the sun so that the small square incisions in the structures that served for windows stood out sharply. There was no movement of any sort, which suggested that the place was uninhabited; indeed, the whole atmosphere suggested desertion, desolation, and decay.

'Well, there it is,' murmured Biggles at last.

'The Lost Oasis,' breathed Kadar.

'It can't be anything else, can it?'

'No. Nothing is shown here on the map.'

Biggles stood up and brushed the worst of the dust from his clothes. 'It's a pity Algy isn't with us,' he said. 'I'm afraid we are in a hopeless mess, and, frankly, I don't see how on earth we are going to get back, but it wouldn't be so bad if we were all together. We've got to make an attempt to find Algy as quickly as we can, that's certain, if for no other reason than that he probably thinks we are dead, whereas we do at least know that he is all right. At any rate, he has enough food and water to last him for some days. The thought that worries me is that he might start off to look for us, in which case he will probably get lost as we did, but without being so lucky as we were in finding water. In fact, I think it is almost a certainty that he will try to find us. Therefore, as I say, we ought to try to get back. All the same, I don't know about you fellows, but I am passing out for want of food, and to start trying to find our way back to the machine in our present state would be dangerous. That village, or whatever it is over there, can't be more than two or three miles away, so I suggest that as a first precaution we go over to it in the hope of finding some sort of food. There will certainly be dates on the trees, and if it is corn growing in those fields, which is what it looks like, then we shall at least be able to keep body and soul together. There should be water there, too. If there isn't, then the only thing we can do is to go back through the cave to where we know there is some. I think we shall have to go back that way in any case. Bats or no bats, it will probably be easier to get through the cave than climb over the top of this hill, which, when the sun gets up, will be pretty nearly red-hot. I'm no mountaineer, anyway. What's your idea of things, Kadar?'

'I agree with you. We must find food before we do anything else. It is dreadful to get weak in the desert: one so soon gives up. I've had some of it, so I know. Let's go across to the oasis and provide ourselves with some dates, if nothing else, and then try to find our way back to Algy. I don't altogether agree with you about the cave, though. This hill behind us is a high one, and it must command a wide view. I would suggest that we attempt to scale it in the hope of seeing from the top the place where we left the machine. If there is no way down the other side, then we shall have to go through the cave whether we like it or not. And as far as getting back to civilization is concerned, I may be wrong, but I have a feeling that the Arabs sometimes come here, although the place may be known only to one or two.'

'What makes you think that?' asked Biggles sharply.

'One thing only: the jewels I told you about. They must come from just such a place as this, and there can't be many such places.'

'Ah, you mean they are found in the – tombs?'

'Yes; jewels are not likely to be found anywhere in Egypt today except in tombs.'

'Well, that's hopeful, anyway,' murmured Biggles. 'But

come on; if we are going across to that village the sooner we start the better, while it is still comparatively cool.'

They set off without delay, but they had not gone far when a crash somewhere above them made them look back. A great stone was bounding down the hill towards them, followed by a number of smaller ones that had evidently been disturbed by its progress.

'Look out!' shouted Biggles, throwing himself flat under an overhanging ledge, and the others crowded into the narrow haven with him.

The stone whirled over their heads and went plunging down into the depths.

'Was that an accident, or is that animated mummy we saw in the cave trying to be unpleasant?' muttered Biggles thoughtfully, as he crawled out of the refuge.

They all stared back up the hill, but there was no sign of life, so, with an occasional apprehensive glance behind them, they resumed their march.

It was soon clear that Biggles had been wrong in his estimate of the distance to the village, for what with the steepness of the hill, and the detours they were often compelled to make round difficult places, they were an hour reaching the bottom, and a further twenty minutes getting to the nearest of the palm-trees; yet the village still looked as far away as when they had started.

'I'm afraid we shall have to alter our plans,' declared Biggles. 'By the time we get to that village it will be too late to think of looking for Algy today. I suggest that we leave the place until later on. We shall have plenty of time to explore it. I can see lots of dates, so let's get a good supply and start back. Another point is, the side of the hill we came down is still in the shade; when the sun gets round a bit, later on, it will be nearly too hot to touch.'

'Yes, I think that's the best plan,' agreed Ginger. 'Let's

get together and muster up all our stores before we start any exploring.'

While they had been talking Kadar had gone on ahead through the trees, and now an excited call sent the others forward at a run. They saw the reason for Kadar's excitement even before they saw him. Set amid the luxuriant palms was a large pool of clear water, gleaming like a mirror.

'This is fine,' declared Biggles enthusiastically, and, lying down at the edge, they all had a long, refreshing drink.

Ginger began stripping off his clothes, an operation which did not take him many seconds, and with a joyous yell he plunged in. But hardly had he struck the water when Biggles, who had sat down to take off his shoes preparatory to following suit, leapt to his feet as white as death.

Ginger's head came to the surface. He was grinning all over his face, and he burbled with his lips to show his contentment.

'Come out!' Biggles's cry was almost a scream.

The expression on Ginger's face altered to one of alarm in an instant, and he struck out swiftly for the bank. He knew Biggles too well to ask questions before obeying, and it was fortunate for him that it was so.

Biggles darted to the water's edge, and whipping out his automatic, endeavoured to get the sight on a long black shadow that was shooting through the water immediately behind Ginger, the displacement of water caused by its passage making a wide ripple on the surface. But he dared not shoot for fear of hitting Ginger, so he could only jump from one foot to the other in his agitation.

Ginger reached the edge of the pool a mere three yards ahead of the thing that was following him. Biggles grabbed him by the arm and literally dragged him out of the water and flung him clear. Then he sprang back himself, while Ginger scrambled madly over the sand away from the death-trap into which he had so light-heartedly jumped.

With the majestic stateliness of a battleship, an enormous crocodile surged up on to the bank and waddled forward several paces on rigid legs before it stopped, its great jaws open, and its crested back arched. And there it stood, blinking with its little eyes at the hastily-retreating airmen, and its massive tail gently stroking the surface of the water.

'Great heaven! What a horror!' gasped Biggles, for the creature was a good twenty feet long. 'How in the name of goodness did a thing like that get here!' He turned wondering eyes to Kadar, who had turned a horrible yellowish-green under his brown skin.

'I should have guessed it,' he answered severely. 'This is quite a common thing. The crocodile played a big part in the religious ceremonies of the ancients in this part of the world, as is shown by many of the old inscriptions and sculptures. Models made of gold have also been found.'

'Well, that puts an end to the bathing party,' muttered Biggles disgustedly, sitting down and fanning his face with his helmet when he saw that the crocodile attempted to come no farther ashore. 'Shall I shoot the brute?' he inquired, looking at Kadar for advice.

'Please yourself. You won't kill him with that pop-gun, though, and there seems to be no object in wounding him. Perhaps it would be better to save what few bullets we have for emergencies. Now that we know that this ugly customer is here it can do us no harm.'

Ginger was putting on his clothes with trembling fingers, regardless of the water that still glistened on his body. He was still pale from shock. 'Let's go back and find Algy,' he said bitterly. 'Scorpions in the sand, crocodiles in the drinking-water, bats in the cave – I shall have bats in the belfry if this goes on.'

Keeping a watchful eye on the monster, Biggles walked farther along the pool and filled the water-bottle with fresh water. 'Let's get some dates,' he suggested dispassionately.

'We shall probably find they've got poisonous bugs in them,' grumbled Ginger. Nevertheless, he swung himself up into a palm that had been blown over at an acute angle by some long-forgotten storm. Not without difficulty, he crawled into the fronds, and from there tossed down several bunches of dates into the waiting hands of those below. This done, they ate as many as they needed, and, each carrying a bunch of the fruit in his left hand, they began retracing their steps.

Ginger turned to where the crocodile was still watching them with an expression suggestive of disappointment on its face, and placing his thumb to his nose, extended his fingers. 'That to you,' he sneered.

Thereafter they began the long climb back up the hill. They started in the shade, but before they reached the entrance to the tombs of the dead the sun was striking the hill-side with its fierce rays. A quick survey disclosed a not-too-difficult way to the top of the hill, so they scrambled on towards the serrated crest that cut into the sky like a row of broken yellow teeth. Biggles was first to reach the top, and, regardless of the heat of the rock, he dropped quickly on his hands and knees when he saw the terrifying abyss that yawned before him. Peering cautiously over the edge, he saw that they were on the top of the cliff immediately above the fissure that gave access to the pool inside, a fact which he was able to ascertain from the position of the 'forest of petrified fungi', and the faint trail of footprints leading from it. All around lay spread out a wild jumble of sun-parched hills, valleys, and gorges, destitute of life, unnerving in their stark barrenness. It reminded Ginger, as he crawled up and looked over the edge, of an enlarged photograph he had once seen of the moon's surface.

Yet in the distance could be seen the end of the rocks and the beginning of the open desert, and Biggles pointed it out. 'Look!' he said. 'There is the palm we nearly hit as we came down. I don't see any palms elsewhere in that direction, so it must be the place.'

'I can't see the machine,' declared Ginger.

'You couldn't expect to,' Biggles told him. 'It was so smothered up with sand that it would be hard enough to see it from a hundred yards, never mind five or six miles. Well, that is the direction we must make for.'

'Yes, that is the palm, without doubt,' put in Kadar. 'You can just see the *wadi* we walked down, this side of it.'

From their bird's-eye view it was, in fact, possible to see the tortured earth in the form of a map, and thus follow with the eyes several routes that would take them back to the place they were so anxious to reach. Biggles took out a pencil, and on one of the few remaining pages of his notebook commenced making a sketch-map, rough, but sufficient for the purpose of finding their way back to the machine. This did not occupy many minutes, and, the task completed, he backed away from the chasm and stood up.

'We can't get down the face of this cliff, that's certain,' he said, 'so, whether we like it or not, we shall have to go back through the cave.'

'What about the bats?' asked Ginger, a trifle nervously.

'We shall have to take our chance with them,' observed Biggles. 'By this time they may have settled down again and be as docile as they were when we first went into the cave. It was that bag of skin and bones that set them on to us, I'm sure.'

'There it goes now. Look!' cried Ginger excitedly, pointing a quivering forefinger at a small, brown, ape-like creature that was scrambling down the hill towards the oasis far beyond the entrance to the tombs.

'I hope he – or she – falls into the pond,' wished Ginger viciously.

'Perhaps it thinks it is following us, not knowing that we came back up here,' suggested Kadar.

'It doesn't matter much what it thinks so long as it keeps out of our way,' said Biggles. 'Frankly, I am glad it is out of the way; there is no knowing what mischief it might be up to if it found us in the cave. The place is unpleasant enough as it is, without any added complications. Come on.'

They made the best speed possible down to the entrance, and the gruesome knowledge of what it held was in some degree compensated for by the cool shade within. Just inside the entrance Biggles mustered his remaining spills, which he had thrust into his pocket when they fled before the bats, and, in spite of Kadar's protests, augmented them with some of his newspaper clippings. Thus provided with means of illumination, they started on their unpleasant journey.

Reaching the tombs, Biggles pointed, without speaking, to the walls, which were festooned with countless sleeping bats, all hanging head downwards. Placing his finger on his lips, he went on through the chamber, and breathed a sigh of relief when they reached the other cave on the opposite side. Along this they hurried, stopping occasionally to light fresh spills, and at length, without incident, they reached the silent pool, now looking indescribably beautiful in a slant of pure white sunshine. There was no sign of the scorpions, which apparently visited the pool only by night – unless it had been, as Kadar had suggested, that they were seeking human flesh – so, after a fortifying drink, they proceeded on the last part of their journey.

With the map to guide them, finding their way through the desolation became a comparatively simple matter, although they took care to mark their trail by dragging their feet through the sand, and sometimes building small cairns with pieces of loose rock.

An hour's steady plodding saw them at the end of the *wadi*, and in their anxiety they traversed it in quick time.

'I don't see him,' said Biggles anxiously, as they approached the machine. Then, raising his voice, 'Hi! Algy!' he called.

There was no answer, so they broke into a run. Panting, they reached the Tourer, still exactly as they had left it, and stared about them.

'Algy!' shouted Biggles again, but only the echoes replied.

Ginger ran to the cabin door and opened it. 'He's not here,' he said. Then he went inside. Presently he returned. 'The rifle's gone,' he said, 'but nothing else seems to have been touched.'

They called again several times, but there was no answering hail, and at length Biggles squatted on one of the under-carriage wheels in the shade afforded by the wings.

'It is as I feared,' he said quietly. 'He's gone. No doubt he went to look for us.'

'Maybe he isn't far away, and will come back presently,' suggested Ginger optimistically.

'That is the best we can hope for,' returned Biggles briefly.

CHAPTER 10

TRAPPED

ALL through the heat of the late afternoon they waited, and experienced for the first time the full force of the desert sun. The sand shimmered and the rocks quivered like live things. The *wadi* became a furnace in which the tortured airmen could only cower under the machine, keeping life in their fast-drying bodies by taking frequent sips of water. As the sun moved round, so they moved with it, in order to keep in the narrow shade provided by the Tourer's wings, augmented by the dust-covers which they brought out of the cabin. Even so, the sand on which the sun had been playing was too hot to touch with the bare hand, and they were compelled to spread about their spare kit and sit on that. Once Ginger, driven to desperation, bolted into the cabin, but he was soon out again, declaring that the heat inside had nearly shrivelled him to a cinder.

'Whether Algy returns or not, we shan't be able to stand much of this,' declared Biggles, during one of the many silences.

'Our skins would soon peel off, and we should probably go blind,' Kadar informed them with disconcerting frankness. 'I have seen —'

'Don't tell us what you've seen,' interrupted Biggles. 'Leave us to guess. It shouldn't be difficult.'

The day wore on, and at long last came the blessed relief of dusk. With many exclamations of thankfulness, they crawled out of their retreat and surveyed the sterile scene.

'If Algy is lost, and has been out all day in that sun without water, he must be a dead man,' declared Biggles disconsolately. 'It's no use blinking at facts. Another hour of it and I should have gone crazy. It is just one of those things one has to experience to believe. I am sorry to say it, but I find it difficult to suppose that Algy will return here. It seems to me that his only chance lay in striking a pool such as we found, or the oasis. Frankly, I don't think it's much good waiting for him. In any case, I don't think we could stand another day like today. It's no use grumbling; we're here, and it looks as though we shall have to spend the rest of our lives here. Has anyone any suggestions to make?'

'The only thing we can do if we wish to remain alive is to go back to the oasis,' declared Kadar emphatically.

'We might have a last look round to see if we can find Algy's tracks,' suggested Ginger. 'It seems like deserting him just to go away.'

'It will be death to remain,' returned Kadar.

'I agree with what you say about desertion, Ginger, but I feel inclined to take Kadar's advice,' said Biggles. 'There's no sense in sitting here and dying by inches while we are within reach of an oasis. We'll have a last look round to see if we can find Algy's tracks, but I don't think we shall, or we should have found them before. If he doesn't come back during the night we'll make for the oasis, starting before dawn. We'll leave some food and water here, of course, on the off-chance that he does come back, and a note saying where we have gone. I'll leave a map, too, showing him how he can find the oasis.'

'That is the most sensible thing to do,' agreed Kadar.

In the fading light they cast about for tracks, but it was

all in vain, and at last, miserable and depressed, they returned to the machine, where Biggles sorted out the meagre store of food and water, and wrote the note to Algy, which he fixed in a conspicuous place on the fuselage. This done, they all lay down to rest and get what sleep they could.

The stars were still shining brightly in the sky when Biggles started making preparations for departure, and the others rose wearily to their feet, conscious for the first time of how much energy had been taken out of them by the lack of normal food and the scorching sun. However, they joined Biggles, who was taking a last look round.

'Ready?' he asked briefly.

'Lead on,' invited Ginger, and they started off on the weary trail back to the oasis.

Fortunately their lassitude wore off as they got into their stride, for the night air was cool and invigorating, and in just over an hour, with the breath-taking desert dawn just breaking, and flooding the hill-tops with its pink radiance, they reached the face of the cliff through which they would have to pass. They approached it cautiously, for they had not forgotten the scorpions. They saw several stray ones, which reared up and waved their tiny but formidable lobster-like claws at them, but there was no mass formation such as they had seen on the occasion of their first visit.

'I should say they scatter to their respective dug-outs as soon as it begins to get light,' opined Biggles. 'Watch your step, everbody. A scorpion sting would just about put the tin hat on things.'

A few stray bats were drifting into the cave, but they did not appear to be vicious, so the airmen ignored them and continued their journey. Biggles had brought with him a good supply of paper, which had been used for wrapping odd articles in the machine, so with a bright torch held aloft they made good progress. There was an anxious moment or two as they passed through the tombs of the dead, for a few of the bats, disturbed, no doubt, by the unusual light, seemed inclined to protest against the intrusion; but the airmen hurried on, and soon found themselves on the side of the hill that overlooked the oasis. They made a thorough scrutiny of the landscape in the hope of seeing Algy before they moved on, but there was no sign of life anywhere, so they set off down the hill.

'I wonder what became of our friend with the wrinkled countenance?' asked Ginger.

'If we see her – I say "her" because I fancy it is a woman – we might try to catch her,' suggested Kadar. 'She ought to be able to tell us something about the place, and whether anybody every comes here.'

'That's a good idea, although I'd as soon try to catch a wild cat,' asserted Biggles, as they approached the pool among the palms, where they proposed to refill the water-bottle, which had been emptied during the march.

Biggles suddenly caught Kadar by the arm. 'I don't think we need find the old hag to ask if anyone comes here,' he said crisply, throwing swift glances to left and right. 'Look! that answers the question. I swear those weren't here yesterday.' He pointed to a group of four marks in the soft sand near the edge of the pool. Unmistakably they had been made by a camel.

Kadar caught his breath sharply, but then nodded as if he understood. 'It is more than likely that they were made by a stray animal,' he said. 'Camels are always wandering away from camps. They have wandered away for thousands of years, yet for some curious reason the Arabs never seem to think of tethering them. Also, a camel can sense water at an enormous distance, and if one is lost anywhere in the district it would make for this pool as a homing pigeon makes for its loft.'

'You know more about this sort of thing than we do, so maybe you are right,' admitted Biggles. 'All the same, we had better keep our eyes skinned. It would be a bad spot to bump into a bunch of Tuareg.'

There was no sign of the dreadful guardian of the pool, so they drank, and after a short rest, during which they ate a few dates, they pushed on towards their objective, wondering what surprises it held in store.

On nearer approach they found that the cacti formed a circular belt just below the summit of the mound on which the village was situated, and so regular was it in its formation that it had obviously been planted by human agency, doubtless as a barrier, in the same way as barbed wire is used in modern warfare. But that, clearly, had been long ago, for much of the monstrous growth was dead and withered, and the airmen had no difficulty in finding a way through it.

'This is the most exciting moment of my life,' announced Kadar, as they approached the grey, weather-worn houses. 'This discovery will cause a tremendous sensation when we get back.'

'*When* we get back,' murmured Biggles dryly.

They soon discovered that the village was, in fact, a citadel, built on the very summit of the mound, with smooth bare walls presented to possible invaders. Unable to find a way up, they could only walk along the base of what was, in effect, a rampart, and in this way they presently came to the entrance which they knew must exist. It was a dark, forbidding portal, medieval in its conception and Moorish in construction, having the customary high, pointed arch.

Biggles looked at Kadar questioningly before going on. 'Don't you think we are taking a bit of a chance, strolling into a place like this without knowing if anyone is inside?' he asked quietly.

'Had there been anyone here they could not have failed to

see us, in which case either they would have come to meet us or prepared a reception, hostile or otherwise. Look at the track. Does it look as if it is ever used? I should say there has been no one here for many years.'

Biggles looked down and saw that what Kadar had said was true. 'What about that corn we saw from the hill-top?' he reminded him.

'If it had once been planted here, and apparently it was, it would go on sowing itself for years,' declared Kadar confidently.

Biggles shrugged his shoulders. 'Well, I suppose you know best,' he said dubiously. 'Anyway, having come so far, we might as well go the whole way. I had a sort of uneasy feeling come over me, that's all.'

Passing through the archway, looking about them expectantly, they found themselves in a wide area, better described, perhaps, as an extensive courtyard, except that it was not paved. It had evidently been a sort of main square, a general assembly place for the people who had once lived there, for a number of crumbling stone seats occurred at intervals around the outside. In the centre was what obviously was the superstructure of a well, and automatically the airmen made their way towards it.

'When you come to think about it, there was bound to be water in here somewhere, otherwise the people could not have survived a siege,' observed Biggles.

But Kadar was not listening. Trembling with excitement, he was examining an inscription which had been carved round the plinth of the wellhead. 'It's Persian!' he exclaimed in a voice vibrant with emotion.

'Never mind about that now; let us go on a bit farther,' suggested Biggles. 'As we are fixed, it looks as if you will have the rest of your life to translate that in.'

Many streets led off the main square, but there was little

to choose between them. None was any wider than a foot-
path. Towards one of these they made their way, often
stepping aside to avoid large colonies of black ants that
hurried about their business. In one place Kadar pointed to
a little snake that lay curled up, watching them with tiny
sparkling eyes.

'Don't step on one of those,' he said earnestly.

'Is it a poisonous sort?' asked Biggles.

'Yes. It's a *nadjda*, the little Egyptian cobra. Some scientists
think that it is the asp with which, it is said, Cleopatra, Queen
of Egypt, committed suicide.'

'You have some pleasant little creatures in this country of
yours, Kadar,' smiled Biggles, as he stepped into the first
house they came to. There was no door, but the remains of
a rush mat, lying where it had fallen, suggested that as a
curtain it had once served the purpose of one.

It was gloomy inside, not that there was very much to see.
A great earthenware jar stood in one corner; beside it was
an old-fashioned flail. A soft thud startled them, but it was
only another *nadjda* that had fallen from the roof. It lay
where it fell, its little forked tongue flicking in and out with
lightning speed.

The airmen looked up. At first they could see nothing but
rotting rafters, made of split palms; but presently, as their
eyes grew accustomed to the dim light, they could make out
a multitude of what looked like little twin stars.

Biggles was the first to realize that they were eyes, and
he stepped back hastily as another *nadjda* thudded to the
floor. 'Great Scott!' he gasped, 'the place is alive with
snakes!'

There was a wild stampede for the door, and the airmen
burst out into the sunshine, where they stood blinking in the
bright light. Then they stiffened, while a strange silence fell.
Standing in a half circle round the doorway were a dozen or

more swathed Tuareg, only their cold, hostile eyes showing above their indigo-tinted veils. There they stood, appraising the airmen with a curious indifference, as they covered them with long, antiquated rifles. Their camels stood in a group near the well, from which direction another figure, draped in an Arab *burnous*, now approached. Pushing his way through the motionless Tuareg, the new-comer threw his *kafieh* aside, disclosing his face. It was Zarwan.

Biggles looked at him. He looked at the rifles covering them, and knew that resistance was useless. One movement towards his pistol would be answered by a dozen rifles – more, in fact, since several other Tuareg were now coming towards the spot.

Zarwan's sleek features broke into a crafty smile, but his eyes were cold. 'So!' he purred, 'we meet again.'

'Well, what about it?' asked Biggles.

Zarwan's smile faded, and his eyes glinted. 'Presently I will show you,' he said smoothly.

'You don't happen to have a drink of water on you, do you?' asked Biggles, who was really thirsty.

Zarwan eyed him malevolently. 'No,' he murmured evenly. 'The first rule in the desert is not to waste water. It would be wasting it to give it to you, for the short time that you will need it.'

'I see,' said Biggles coolly, his eyes flashing round the Tuareg, who, while Zarwan was speaking, had been edging nearer. Then he shrugged his shoulders, realizing that resistance would be tantamount to suicide, for the muzzles of a score of rifles were almost touching him. As a result of experience, he was a firm believer in the old adage, 'While there is life there is hope', and he could see no point in throwing away their lives uselessly. His common sense told him that they would be riddled with bullets before they could even draw their weapons. He did not, of course, know

Zarwan's methods, or it may have been that he would have chosen this course.

The Tuareg made a sudden rush, and rough hands were laid on them. Kadar, perhaps suspecting what was in store for them, made a gallant but foolish attempt to break free, but he went down under a hail of blows. As he fell he shouted something evidently intended for Biggles's and Ginger's benefit, but in his excitement he lapsed into his own tongue, and so the warning passed unheeded.

Leather cords, such as those used for securing baggage on camels, were slipped over their wrists and ankles, and presently they all lay on the ground, trussed like fowls prepared for the oven, and as helpless.

Zarwan pushed his way to the front and smiled down at them, kicking Biggles in the ribs as he spoke in his soft, sibilant voice. 'So I am the oily-faced hog?' he sneered. 'You thought you could threaten me.' His voice rose to a thick husky note as his temper got the better of him, and little flecks of foam appeared at the corners of his mouth. Then, suddenly, as if he could not bear to delay his revenge a moment longer, he said something swiftly to the Arabs in a language neither Biggles nor Ginger understood, although Kadar may have done.

Instantly the three of them were seized and dragged to the centre of the courtyard where, with the Tuareg chattering like a lot of excited monkeys, their bonds were removed and readjusted. Camel pegs were driven into the ground, four to each of them, and to these their wrists and ankles were made fast so that they lay on their backs in the position known as spreadeagled.

Biggles bit his lip, regretting bitterly that he had not chosen the easier way out, but even then he did not know the worst. A grinning Arab appeared with a small goatskin in his hand, from the mouth of which oozed a sticky substance.

Kadar knew only too well what was happening, for the torture of the ants is as old as the very hills in Egypt and the Sudan.

'It is wild honey,' he muttered hoarsely. 'They lay a trail of it to an ants' nest. It —' There came the sound of a blow and his voice ended abruptly.

Biggles ground his teeth, as much with impotent fury as fear, but he was powerless.

Their work complete, the Tuareg, with Zarwan slightly in front, formed a rough circle round their victims and prepared to watch their death agonies.

A moment later something nipped Biggles's ankle so sharply that, unprepared as he was, he winced, and jerked his leg violently but uselessly against its peg – an involuntary movement that brought a rasping laugh from Zarwan. Biggles felt the insect that had bitten him crawling up his leg, but already his brain was reeling from the blinding glare of the sun.

'Don't worry, you fellows,' he said quietly, 'it will soon be over.'

CHAPTER 11

WHAT HAPPENED
TO ALGY

IF the previous twenty-four hours had been full of adventures for Biggles and his two companions, Algy had also had his share; perhaps more than his share, for, being alone, he had no one to consult, in addition to which, as Biggles had feared, he had been consumed with anxiety on their behalf.

After watching Biggles and the others out of sight up the *wadi*, he had returned to the machine to kill time as well as he could pending their return. He cleaned the rifle and got out a few clips of cartridges, not for any definite reason, but in order to be ready in the unlikely event of their being needed. Then he lay down under the wing to rest.

Utter silence reigned. With his chin cupped in the palms of his hands, he stared at the colourless landscape around him, an undulating expanse of grey without anywhere offering rest for the eyes. There was no definite configuration, no scene to remember; nothing to break the monotony of rock and sand. A brooding, indefinable atmosphere of remote antiquity dominated everything, as if the overwhelming solitude was peopled by the spirits of a long-forgotten past. The only thing that moved was the sun, and from time to time Algy was compelled to change his position to keep clear of its burning rays.

The time passed slowly; how slowly he did not know, for his watch had stopped and he was too tired to look at the watch on the instrument-board. Once or twice he nearly dozed, but, remembering his duty, he forced himself to keep awake.

He was not conscious of the moment when he first began to feel uneasy. He stared up the *wadi*, wishing his companions would come back, for he felt that the breathless hush was getting on his nerves. Then he realized that he had been watching for them for some time, and that he was getting worried, and with the knowledge a sudden pang of anxiety swept over him. Could anything have happened? It hardly seemed possible. There was just a chance, of course, that they might lose their way, but Biggles was not the sort of fellow to do that. Thus he comforted himself, but still they did not come. Once a distant echo reached his ears, but it was so faint that he could not make out what it was, nor could he locate the direction from which it had come, and in the end he dismissed it from his mind, putting the cause down to a piece of falling rock.

But when the sun began to sink over the skyline of the distant hills, and still they had not returned, his anxiety grew to real alarm; not only on their account, but on his own, for he knew that he would not be able to endure the solitude alone without going mad. He climbed the nearest hill, but could see nothing of them. He shouted, and listened for a reply, but none came – except the mocking echoes. Depressed, he returned to the machine, wondering if he ought to go to look for them. It was a difficult problem. If he left the spot, and they returned during his absence, they would probably go off to look for him. After that anything might happen. Both he and the others might wander about the hills until they died from exhaustion without finding each other again.

Came night, and he sat down on one of the undercarriage wheels to wait, but he could not remain still. He drank sparingly of the water, ate a biscuit or two, and then paced up and down. The hours went by, each one as it passed leaving him more and more depressed. The silence was awful. The desert was awful. Everything was awful, he decided miserably. What fools they had been to listen to the crazy young Egyptian and his crazy scheme. Thus he thought bitterly as he paced up and down the deserted *wadi*. No longer did he attempt to deceive himself. Something must have happened. Not willingly would they have left him for so long.

His heart gave a great leap as a distant sound reached his ears. At last! Yet, strangely enough, the sound seemed to come from the desert and not from the far end of the *wadi*. For what purpose could they have gone into the desert? It was absurd. Nothing could have induced them to go out into that dreadful waste of sand. Again the sound reached his ears, and he knew beyond doubt that it could only have been made by a human being. Grabbing the rifle, he ran down the *wadi* towards the open sand, and then climbed up on a piece of rock in order to get a wider view.

The sight that met his gaze was so unexpected that at first he thought the desert was playing tricks with his eyes. In the bright moonlight, moving slowly in single file towards the hills, and not more than two or three miles away, was a long line of camels. A caravan!

His first impulse was to rush out and hail it, but then he remembered the Tuareg and hung back in a quandary. If the new-comers were the dreaded desert warriors it were better to keep clear of them, he thought. Had Kadar been there it would have been different, for he was, after all, of the country, and he could speak their language. He might have arranged with them to take a message to Siwah, or some such place. But in the circumstances it would be asking for trouble to expose himself, a hated *roumi*, to them. Yet suppose it was a proper caravan? To let it disappear might be to lose a chance that would not occur again. It was very hard to know what to do for the best.

In the end he decided on a sort of compromise. The best plan, he thought, was, as a first precaution, to try to find out who the riders were, after which he would know better what to do. There was plenty of cover, and in any case they would hardly be expecting anyone in such a place. So, with this scheme in view, taking care to keep out of sight, he began walking along the fringe of the rocks on a course that would intercept the caravan when it reached the hills. It was an eerie experience, this stalking of mysterious black shadows in the moonlight, and more than once he wished fervently that the others were with him.

It was while he was creeping round a buttress of rock that he found the lance. It gave him a queer shock. He had been compelled to round the buttress for the reason that a hill towered high at that point, and it would have been dangerous, if not impossible, to climb it. Keeping close to the still-warm rock, he saw the point of something sticking out of the sand just in front of him. At first he thought it was a twig, but an instant later he realized that that was impossible, for where there were no trees there could be no twigs. Putting out his hand, he touched it, and then he knew at once what it was. Slowly he allowed his hand to slide down the point, and the carved metal-work touched a chord in his memory. The lance was buried deeply, so deeply that little more than the point protruded, for the sand had silted up around it, which no doubt accounted for its remaining in such a position. He did not know, of course, that the weapon he was feeling had once belonged to Mazeus, son of Hystomannus; or that his was the first hand to touch it since that fatal night, more than two thousand five hundred years before, when the *haboob*

had overtaken Cambyses' army. But he remembered vaguely
what Kadar had said about a lance, and realized that by an
amazing chance he had stumbled on the same weapon.
Still, he could do nothing about it now, for the caravan had
nearly reached the hills, and he had to hurry to be in time to
intercept it.

He reached the spot for which the caravan was obviously
making, a clearly defined pass, almost like a dried-up water-
course, and he was at once struck by the significance of the
fact that if the caravan knew so exactly where to enter the
hills, at least one of the party must have been there before.
It rather looked as if the hills were on a regular caravan
route, after all, and but for the incident of the spear he would
have dismissed the possibility of their having arrived at the
long-lost Oasis of Zenzura.

He had little time to ponder the matter now, however, for by
this time the caravan was almost upon him, and he crouched
behind a rock to watch it pass, hoping that by some word
or sign the errand on which it was bound, or its leadership,
would be revealed to him. Nor was he disappointed, for
although the line of shrouded figures, some twenty in all,
with two men riding side by side at the head, filed past without a sound, he learned two things. At first his discovery
filled him with dismay, but this was soon replaced by fierce
satisfaction.

He saw at once that the night riders were Tuareg. The veils
they wore over the lower part of their faces told him that.
There was nothing remarkable about the leaders, but the last
seven riders in the line were each leading another camel which
was heavily loaded. Not that this struck him as unusual. It
was the last led camel of all that caused him to catch his
breath, thrilling under the shock of his discovery. For he had
seen it before. It was a light fawn in colour, with a peculiar
white stocking on the near foreleg. When Kadar had bought

the camels for the caravan Algy had been with him, and just such an animal had been among those he had bought. It seemed impossible that there could be two camels marked in such an unusual way. Then, in a flash, he understood everything. The Tuareg were those who had raided their caravan, murdered their drivers and stolen their stores. The tracks of the raiders had led in a southerly direction. The Tourer had been blown south by the *haboob*, which had no doubt delayed the caravan. Everything fitted perfectly.

This discovery threw Algy's brain into such a state of chaos that for a few moments he could not see the vital facts of the situation in their true perspective. They altered everything. But as he sat and wrestled with the problem, certain predominating factors emerged. In the first place, the raiders represented a new and hitherto unsuspected danger, one of which Biggles and the others would be unaware. If they were still alive it was not unlikely that they would encounter the caravan, with disastrous results. Again, when the raiders had left the scene of the massacre they had taken the petrol with them. They had also taken the stores, but these paled into insignificance beside the petrol, which was the one thing that could get them back to civilization. There was, he realized, a chance that the Tuareg had unburdened themselves of the petrol, but this seemed unlikely, for had the mere destruction of the spirit been their object they could have pierced the cans as they lay on the ground, and thus settled the business there and then. No, he decided; the obvious inference was that if they had taken the petrol in the first place they still had it with them, although what they proposed to do with it he could not imagine. He spent several seconds thinking about this, for it was the weakest link in his chain of deduction, but the solution baffled him. A little later, when he did know, he realized that had he spent the rest of his life thinking about it he would not have guessed the answer.

By this time the tail of the caravan had disappeared round a bend in the pass, and he emerged from his hiding-place torn by indecision. If only Biggles and the others had been there! Petrol had arrived in a way that on the face of it seemed little short of miraculous, although it was, in fact, due to a perfectly natural sequence of events. What ought he to do? What would Biggles do in such circumstances?

The trouble with Algy was that he wanted to do two things at once – to be in two places at once. He wanted to rush back to the machine to see if Biggles had returned, and he wanted to follow the caravan, fearing that it might disappear in the hills. It must be remembered that he had no idea of how far they stretched. In the end he decided to follow the caravan, anyhow until it made camp. With the camp marked down he would then dash back to the machine and tell the others – assuming that they had returned – what had happened. If they had not returned – well, in that case he did not know what he would do. He would have to decide whether to go in search of them and abandon the petrol, or return to the caravan in the hope of making contact with them later.

His feet making no sound on the sand, he set off up the path in the tracks of the camels, scouting each corner carefully before rounding it. It was nerve-trying work, for the pass was in deep shadow, and the camels travelled so noiselessly that he was terrified that they might stop and he would blunder into them. Presently, however, the sides of the pass fell away so that it became a shallow *wadi* into which the moon penetrated, and he was able to see his quarry some distance ahead. Keeping in the shadows on the edge of the valley, he hurried on after it. Would it never halt? Hour after hour it went on until he began to regret his decision to follow it. The thought of the long journey back appalled him, but it was no use thinking of turning back now. He had come so far that it would be galling to have to give up. He had expected it to halt any minute, and he still expected it to, but the night was far advanced when, to his unspeakable relief, he saw the camels standing in a group in the centre of a small cup-shaped depression. Watching from a distance, he saw them 'couch' and saw the Arabs unloading them.

Again he was worried by indecision. Should he start back at once, or should he try to approach nearer? But for the petrol he would not have hesitated. He would have gone straight back. But the most vital question of all could still not be answered with certainty. Had the Tuareg got the petrol with them or had they discarded it? In the end he decided that he ought to find out, and with this object in view he crept forward.

The place was strewn with rocks of all shapes and sizes, so there was really very little risk of being seen, and as there was still sand underfoot there was little likelihood of his being heard. He also gathered confidence from the fact that the Arabs would not suspect that they were being watched in such a remote place, so it was extremely unlikely that they would post a guard or even keep a look-out.

Comforting himself with this thought, he advanced, and was soon as near as he dare approach. The Tuareg had lighted a small fire with the fuel they invariably carried with them, and around this they were sitting in a rough circle. Suddenly one of them laughed, and the sound was so unexpected that Algy stared in amazement. Somehow he could not imagine a Tuareg laughing. The mutter of their deep guttural voices reached him. They seemed to be in good spirits. He saw one reach forward and pick up what was unmistakably a two-gallon petrol can, and that told him what he was so anxious to learn. They still had the petrol with them. But what was the fellow doing with the can – with the petrol? Then, to his utter and complete astonishment, he saw the can being passed round. They were drinking from it!

When he recovered from his astonishment his first feeling, not unnaturally, was one of intense disappointment and mortification. Not because they were drinking the precious petrol. His common sense refused to believe that anyone in his right mind drank petrol. Clearly, therefore, they had thrown the petrol away, and were using the cans for the transport of water. So certain was he of this that he was about to retire, when one of the Arabs, after drinking from the can, spat deliberately into the fire. There was a shout of laughter as a tongue of flame spurted upward, curled in the air for a moment and then died down again. Algy's spirits soared with the flame, for it told him that, incredible though it appeared, the ignorant savages were actually drinking petrol.[1] Whether they drank it because they liked the taste of it, whether they really thought that it was a white man's beverage, or whether, knowing what it was, they drank it simply in order to intoxicate themselves, he neither knew nor cared. As far as he was concerned the only thing that mattered was that the petrol was there, and if the silly fools drank themselves into unconsciousness, so much the better. They would be a lot less formidable in that condition, anyway, he thought, not without satisfaction; and when, presently, one of them got up and staggered about – nearly falling into the fire – he knew beyond all doubt that what he hoped had come to pass. The petrol was there; not necessarily all of it, but there was at least some, and in their condition it was more precious than gold.

Another one stood up, a short man, dressed rather differently from the others in that he wore a *kafieh*, the normal Arab head-dress, which is a strip of linen bound around the crown by a piece of rope, or gold thread, according to rank. He watched him toss the *kafieh* aside as though he found it

---

[1] Drinking petrol is a very common practice with native races in many parts of the world.

irritating, and for a moment the orange glow of the fire played on his face. Algy recognized him at once. It was Zarwan.

To say that he was astounded is to put it mildly. He was staggered. He had almost forgotten the man's existence, and to find him in such a place, at such a time, and with such companions, completely bewildered him, for it put the whole situation on a different footing.

This condition did not last long, however, and as soon as he had recovered his wits he began to back away. At all costs Biggles must know of this, he decided, and without further delay.

Once in the shadow of the pass, he broke into a trot, a pace that he maintained until, just as the dawn was breaking, he arrived back at the machine. One glance was enough. They were not there. They were, it will be recalled, just bursting out of the tombs of the dead, pursued by the bats, but, of course, he knew nothing about that. He only knew that they were not there. Exhausted and sick at heart, he flung himself down to rest, and to think.

CHAPTER 12

ALGY TO THE RESCUE

A DEATHLY hush settled over everything, yet still he sat there, no longer daring to hope, hardly daring to contemplate his plight; for thus does the unutterable silence of the desert corrode the will to live, even as the drifting sand wears away the rocks until they, too, become sand. After a time he lay down, and, later, must have dozed, for it was broad daylight when he returned to consciousness.

Springing to his feet, he looked about him wildly, but the scene was just the same. Nothing moved. The pleasant dawn-wind had gone, and the silence was so intense that it worried his ear-drums. A dreadful feeling crept over him that he was alone in the world; that a calamity had befallen it, leaving him the only creature alive. He tried to dismiss the thought, knowing that madness lay that way, the fatal mental state which the French desert troops, the Foreign Legion, and the Bataillon d'Afrique call *le cafard*, but it persisted. In any case, he thought, it was no use waiting any longer. It would be better to follow the caravan while he still had his wits, in the hope that it would lead him to an oasis, or, at least, a water-hole. Anything was better than sitting by the silent machine. There was just a chance, too, if he followed the caravan, that he might find an opportunity to recover some of the petrol, even a little – enough to allow him a few minutes' flight. Ten minutes in the air would be more likely to reveal the others, dead or alive, than a month of searching on foot.

Thus decided, he slung a water-bottle over his shoulder, put a few biscuits in his pocket, and, picking up the rifle, set off towards the pass where the caravan had entered the hills. Had he known that the others, at that particular moment, were hurrying back from the oasis towards the *wadi*, this story would have had a different ending; but he did not, so he trudged along, forcing himself to keep going in spite of an insidious voice that whispered to him to give up, that his effort would be in vain.

The heat became torture as the sun climbed majestically towards its zenith, unmindful of the little figure that plodded wearily along the foot of the rocks, sometimes sinking down to escape the fierce rays whenever scant shade offered itself, not only to escape the glare, but to gain a brief respite from the burning sand.

It was his feet that worried Algy most. The sand was so hot that he appeared to be walking over a furnace, and the pain was most unbearable. He did not know that even Arabs will refuse to step out into the open during the heat of the day, on account of the discomfort caused to the feet.

However, he reached the lance, and, dragging it from its resting-place, crawled into the cavity where, two thousand five hundred years before, Mazeus had crept in to die. And so he found him, the pathetic sun-bleached bones showing here and there through the joints of the ancient armour.

Algy did not stay long. The relic was too grim a reminder of what was likely to be his own fate; so he drank a little water and hurried on, using the lance as a staff, unconcerned with the importance of his find. He was concerned only with the present, not with the past.

The going was not quite so bad in the pass, for under the eastern wall there was still a little shade, and he made the most of it, striding along with dogged determination, but realizing more and more that he had been unwise to start such a journey in the heat of the day. Still, as he had started he might as well go on, he thought miserably.

It was twilight when he came to the place where the caravan had halted the previous night, for in spite of his determination he had found it necessary to halt and rest occasionally. With thoughtful eyes he surveyed the scene. All that remained was a dead fire and two empty petrol-cans. He was not surprised, for he had not supposed that the sun-parched depression was the caravan's final destination. The camel-tracks were plain enough in the sand, showing which way they had gone, and he was not a little concerned to note that they led away into the very heart of the hills. For a few minutes he regarded them wearily, sick at heart, realizing that he could not hope to overtake the caravan that day. He was, in fact, physically and mentally worn out, and as it was now nearly dark, he decided that his best plan would be to pass the night where he was.

Scooping a hole for his hip, and piling up the sand to form a pillow, he lay down, and so exhausted was he that, in spite of his discomfort and anxiety, he was soon asleep. Nor did he awake, until the dawn-wind fanned his brow.

Refreshed, he sat up, drank a little water, and then, picking up his things, set off once more on the trail of the caravan, little dreaming that Biggles and the others were, at that precise moment, turning their backs on the Tourer and starting off down the *wadi*.

The pleasant conditions of dawn were short-lived. In a little while the sun flamed up above the hill-tops, and the dreaded heat came again to torture him. Inevitably his stride shortened, but he struggled on, with the hoof-marks of the camels now dancing before his eyes.

The trail seemed interminable as hour after hour he

dragged his protesting body through a shimmering nightmare-world of heat and desolation. Would it never end? More than once he was on the point of giving up, almost overwhelmed by a sense of hopeless futility. He felt that he had been marching for weeks instead of hours; he had no idea of how far he had travelled, for time and distance had become meaningless.

He was nearly at the end of his endurance, and he was swaying as he walked, when, rounding a heat-distorted mass of rock, he saw the thing he had begun by hoping to find, but had long since dismissed from his thoughts: an oasis. At first he could not believe it, so unreal did the green palms look after the colourless wilderness through which he had passed; but when at last he convinced himself that it was really there, he took a good drink of water and strode on with renewed vigour.

The oasis was, he judged, not more than two miles away, but in this, like Biggles, he was mistaken, for it took him nearly an hour to reach it. On his right rose a towering hill, but he paid little attention to it, being more concerned with the oasis and the village which he now saw behind it.

As he neared the motionless palms, he began to move with more caution, realizing that the caravan had probably halted in their shade. Dodging from cover to cover, he approached, and he soon saw that there was good ground for his suspicions. Camels were standing among the trees, but all seemed very quiet, so, with the stealth of a Red Indian on the war-path, he crept nearer.

Presently he saw the pool, and passed his tongue over his dry lips at the thought of burying his face in the cool water. But this was a pleasure in which he could not immediately indulge, for lying near the edge were two Tuareg, asleep, judging by their attitudes. Several camels browsed in the palms behind them, beside their loads, which included the petrol-cans.

For some minutes he watched the two Arabs, but when they did not move he decided to take a chance. Creeping round to the opposite side of the pool, he wormed his way forward until he could reach the water; then, unslinging his water-bottle, he held it under the surface until it was full.

Still the Arabs did not move, so, emboldened by his success, he crept nearer, and was about to plunge his face into the water when an incident occurred that caused an abrupt change in his plan. The water on the far side of the pool parted as a long black object broke the surface and surged towards the sleeping men. He saw at once that it was an enormous crocodile, and he sprang back into the trees in a panic, fearing that there might be more.

In that brief moment the dreadful thing had happened. The crocodile, moving at a speed that he would not have imagined possible, dashing forward, and its huge jaws closed over the legs of the nearest Tuareg.

In a split second all was uproar and confusion. The doomed man let out a scream of terror, and clawed madly at the sand over which he was now being dragged towards the pool. He might as well have clutched at the air for all that it helped him. His companion seemed to lose his head. Aroused suddenly from a heavy sleep, at first he could only dash up and down shouting at the top of his voice; then, seeing that this was likely to be of no avail, he rushed into the trees and returned an instant later with a rifle. Hardly pausing to take aim, he blazed into the flying spray at the edge of the pool.

Whether the shot had any effect on either man or beast Algy did not wait to see, for, ricocheting off the water, it came near to hitting him, and he darted out of the line of fire. Vaguely he had wondered what had become of the rest of the caravan, and the crashing report answered the question for him, for, from the near distance – from the village, it

seemed – came answering shouts. He waited for no more, but
with the lance and water-bottle in one hand, and the rifle in
the other, he made off as fast as his legs could carry him.
Where he was going he did not know, for the palms obstructed
his view. Not that he cared particularly; his one idea was to
place himself as quickly as possible some distance from the
pool, so that the other Tuareg, whom he could now hear
running down the hill from the village, would not discover
him. For a good ten minutes he ran, and then, hearing no
sound of pursuit, he paused to recover his breath. A short
distance away a tiny white object caught his eye, and he
picked it up curiously, wondering what it could be. It was,
he found, a piece of paper, but it was not that fact alone that
made him drop his weapons and stare at it in dumb amazement. There was printing on it, and the words were in English.
Reading them, he perceived that what he held was a fragment
of one of the old newspapers that had been used to wrap up
certain of their stores. The significance of it was not lost on
him; he knew that the others must have been there, and that
with food and water available they should still be alive.

Gone now was the old lethargy, and he looked eagerly to
right and left in the hope of finding another clue. Seeing
nothing of the kind, however, he turned his interest to his
surroundings, and observed that he was on the edge of the
oasis on the side nearest to the village. No one was in sight,
and a babble of voices from the direction of the pool told
him the reason: the Tuareg had forgathered there. Where
were Biggles and the others? Where had they gone after
leaving the oasis? With the Tuareg about, it seemed hardly
likely that they could still be in it. Had they gone back to the
machine, assuming that they knew the way, or had they gone
up to the village? The latter seemed most likely; in any case,
it seemed fairly certain that they would go and explore it
before returning to the machine. His best plan, he decided,

was to do the same thing. If he did not find them in the village then he would return to the original rendezvous.

Making a wide detour that took him some distance round the hill, to a position where he could not be seen from the pool, he began his arduous ascent, beating off the flies that swarmed around his head. He could see no sign of a gateway, but following the wall as the others had done, although some distance from the point where they had struck it, he found a place where the rampart had crumbled, and up this, not without difficulty, he made his way.

Clambering down over the falling stones on the inside of the wall, he found himself in a narrow, deserted street, but there appeared to be an open space at the far end, for he could see the white sunlight blazing down into it. Still using the lance as a staff, in which capacity he had found it very useful, and with the rifle under his left arm, he made his way quietly down the street, keeping a sharp watch for signs of the others, but little dreaming of the spectacle that awaited him at the end. Alert for danger, he peeped round the corner into the square.

He must have remained motionless, staring, for a good half minute, while his eyes conveyed to his brain the almost unbelievable truth; and it was only Kadar's voice, raving in delirium, that finally spurred him to action.

In the centre of the square, not more than a score of paces away, lay three figures which he recognized at once, although the grim details were not immediately apparent. Standing near them, with their backs towards him, were three Tuareg, rifles under their arms. A short distance away a small group of camels patiently awaited their owners' pleasure.

Algy realized that a few moments before all the Tuareg must have been there, but the diversion caused by the crocodile had sent most of them rushing down to the pool to see what was the matter; and, needless to say, he was more than thankful that it was so, for he had no delusions about the fighting qualities of the Tuareg, and the three who had evidently been left on guard over the prisoners were likely to prove a formidable nut to crack.

His opening move was not very successful. Leaning the lance against the wall in order to leave his hands free, he took aim at the nearest Tuareg, for he knew that the only arguments the desert nomads understood were bullets and cold steel, and any other method of approach would be mere foolishness. So he prepared forthwith to reduce the number of his opponents to two.

But there is much truth in old proverbs, and the one about 'many a slip 'twixt the cup and the lip' is no exception. In this case it was the lance that slipped, and even as his finger was tightening on the trigger, it slid down the wall and struck the ground with a crash.

The Tuareg, who by their very natures are always alert for danger, whirled round at the precise moment that Algy's rifle cracked, with the result that the bullet missed its mark. Dropping on to one knee, he jerked another cartridge into the breech, and by that time the Tuareg were halfway towards him. The rifle spat again, and this time there was no mistake; the leading Arab crashed forward into the dust. One of the others fired as he ran; the bullet smashed against the wall near Algy's face, and the sting of the soft lead, some of which splashed against his shoulder, nearly knocked him over. He fired again, and the second Arab went down, but he was only wounded, and was soon on his knees, still holding his rifle.

But Algy was now in evil case, for the last Tuareg was on him. Fortunately, as it happened, he was the man who had already discharged his weapon, but, whirling it round, he prepared to use the butt. Algy made a desperate attempt to get another cartridge into the breech, but his haste was his undoing, and, in attempting to close the bolt before the cartridge was in line, the weapon jammed. There was no time to clear it. Springing to his feet, he swung it above his head to protect himself from the other's flailing butt. He was only just in time. The big, old-fashioned weapon came down with a crash across his own, splintering to pieces under the impact and knocking him over backwards.

In an instant the Tuareg had whipped out a long, curved knife, and with his evil, pock-marked face grinning with savage delight, he leapt forward to drive the weapon home. Algy twisted like an eel as he endeavoured to thrust himself to one side, and his hand closed over the haft of the lance. Acting now under the sheer impulse of self-preservation, he jerked the weapon up just as the Tuareg flung himself on him. The point of Mazeus's lance never found a more fatal mark; it caught the Tuareg squarely in the throat and impaled him as cleanly as a butterfly is impaled upon a pin.

Exerting all his strength, Algy flung the weapon sideways, and the Tuareg with it, for he had seen that he was by no means out of danger. The fellow he had wounded had levelled his rifle, and he leapt aside as the weapon roared. The bullet whistled past his face, and the Arab, seeing that he had missed, drew his dagger.

Algy did not hesitate. He took out his automatic and deliberately shot the savage dead. For a moment he stood swaying while he recovered from the shock; then, snatching up the dagger that lay near his feet, he ran forward, cold with the fear that he might be too late. He reached Biggles first, and shuddered as he saw the broad, black line of ants hurrying towards him.

Biggles was far gone, but he managed to smile, and whisper 'Good boy.'

In four swift slashes Algy had cut him free. Unslinging the water-bottle, he thrust it into his hands. Then he cut the thongs that held the others, by the end of which time Biggles was sitting up, drinking.

Algy did not stay. For all he knew there were other Tuareg near at hand and, being a soldier, his first thought was the consolidation of their position. 'Look after the others,' he shouted at Biggles, and then dashed back to his fallen rifle. It took him a moment to clear the jam, and this done, he ran to the gateway, prepared to hold it until Biggles was able to take charge. To his relief he saw that the hill-side was clear, although two or three Arabs, no doubt alarmed by the shots, had run out from the trees and were staring up the track. Others joined them, and they began to run forward, so he dashed back to inform Biggles of the circumstances.

Biggles and Ginger, he was relieved to find, were already on their feet and helping Kadar, who was sitting up, although clearly in a bad way. Not that Biggles or Ginger were themselves normal; Biggles's lips were bleeding, and Ginger had a bad sun-blister on the side of his face; also he still seemed somewhat dazed. Kadar appeared to be suffering chiefly from shock; his eyes rolled and he rambled incoherently, although with each gulp of water he seemed to improve. They all suffered more or less from ant bites, but they were not serious, for the main body of the ants had not quite reached the spot.

'You were just about in time,' Biggles told Algy in a brief aside, while he brushed several ants from his person. 'Another five minutes and we were goners. What is happening down below?'

'The Tuareg are on their way back – to see what the shots were about, I suppose.'

'Somebody fired a shot down by the pool; it was that and somebody shouting that sent them rushing down there,' Biggles told him. 'Was that anything to do with you?'

'No. I'll tell you about it later on. What are we going to do – try to hold the gate?'

'I don't think so. It is as hot as Hades up there, and the place is alive with poisonous snakes, anyway. I haven't had time to think properly yet, but the first thing we must do is to make ourselves scarce, and leave that swine Zarwan and his toughs wondering where we have gone. Did you know he was here?'

'Yes, and they've still got the petrol with them. I'll tell you all about it as soon as we get clear. The street I came down is the best way for us to go, I think, because there is a breach in the wall through which we can get clear of the town.' Algy spoke rapidly, knowing that their position was still desperate.

'All right,' agreed Biggles. 'You get the others into it, while I try to hold up the Tuareg. Grab a water-skin off one of those camels and take any weapons that are likely to be useful.' With that he took the rifle out of Algy's hands and hurried across to the gateway.

CHAPTER 13

CAPTURED

ALGY managed to get Ginger and Kadar into the shade of
the narrow street down which he had come, and the sight of
the lance seemed to bring Kadar round to normal more
quickly than the water had done.

'Where did that come from?' he gasped.

'I found it in the desert,' Algy told him, as he recovered the
weapon.

'It's Persian work,' cried Kadar. 'I hope you remember
where you found it.'

'We'll talk about that later on, if you don't mind,' suggested Algy. 'We're not out of the wood yet – or rather, the
village. The Tuareg are on our track. Hark at that,' he went
on, as Biggles's rifle cracked twice in quick succession. 'He
wouldn't use ammunition at that rate if things weren't getting hot. Come on; we must keep going.'

They reached the spot where the wall had broken down,
and there, a few minutes later, Biggles joined them.

'Where are we bound for?' he asked quickly. 'We've no
time to waste. Those black devils are crawling up the hill
under cover of the rocks; they'll be at the gate in a minute or
two.'

'From where they are they will not be able to see us if we
go out this way,' declared Algy. 'We're too far round the

corner. I vote that we evacuate the place and try to find a
hide-up in that corn down below. That will at least give us
time to get our breath and make some sort of plan. Zarwan
is bound to think we are still in the village, and will probably
spend some time looking for us.'

'That sounds a sensible idea to me,' agreed Biggles, 'although I am tempted to wait and try to get a shot at that
murdering villain Zarwan. Still, that will come in time, no
doubt. Perhaps we had better get down below. I am anxious
to hear about this petrol.'

Without any further waste of time they made their way
down over the fallen boulders of which the wall had been
built, and, hurrying on, at length came to rest in the welcome
shade of a spreading fig-tree that stood at the junction of the
belt of prickly pear and a wide expanse of maize.

'Now then,' said Biggles, sitting down at the foot of the
tree. 'Cut out the details; what about the petrol?'

In as few words as possible, yet omitting nothing of importance, Algy told the others his story; of how he had seen
the caravan coming out of the desert, and his subsequent
discovery of the petrol. He also told them about that
affair at the pool when the Tuareg had been seized by the
crocodile.

'We all know about that gentleman,' declared Biggles
grimly, referring, of course, to the crocodile. 'He jolly nearly
got Ginger.'

'What on earth happened to you?' asked Algy. 'Why
didn't you come back to the machine?'

'We got lost,' replied Biggles tersely. 'As a matter of fact,
we did find our way back to the machine at the finish, only
to discover that you weren't there. We couldn't stand the
heat, so we decided to go back to the oasis which we had
found – the one down below. We left a note for you pinned
on the fuselage, saying that we had been back and had gone

again, with a map showing you how the oasis could be found.'

'When was that?'

'This morning. We left the machine at dawn.'

'Ah! I haven't been back to the machine since then, so I didn't find the note. I spent last night in the desert.'

'I see,' nodded Biggles. 'We haven't time to discuss these things now; the one thing that really matters above everything else is the petrol. If we can get it, it answers all the questions in front of us. We should then be able to get away, and deal with Zarwan in our own time. By jove! I believe we could do it. How many Tuareg do you reckon there were altogether when you first saw them, Algy?'

'Twenty.'

'Very well. You got three. The croc. got one, and I just plugged one from the gate – that leaves fifteen, and there must be very nearly that number now storming up to the gate. If a guard has been left over the petrol and stores it can't be more than two or three men, and we should be a match for them.'

'But we couldn't carry all that petrol,' said Algy wonderingly.

'I know we couldn't, but with luck we might be able to hide it. If we could find a hole in the sand – and I seem to remember seeing several that would do – we could put the cans into it and cover them up. How we should get it again is something I can't answer, but while it exists there is always a chance that we might, which is more than can be said once it is drunk or destroyed. It might be a thousand years before any more petrol is brought here, and that is a bit too long for us to wait. I'd rather throw the cans into the pond, crocodile or no crocodile, than Zarwan should have it. He thinks we're still in the village, so, as I see it, this is an opportunity that may never occur again. It is a risky business, I know, but I am game to try it if anyone else is.'

Algy and Ginger agreed promptly; and so, for that matter, did Kadar, but he was in no condition to fight, so Biggles told him to keep close behind them, carrying the water-supply.

Mustering their weapons, they found that they had the rifle, with six rounds of ammunition, Algy's automatic, a loaded Tuareg rifle, two daggers, and the lance. Biggles's, Ginger's, and Kadar's automatics had, of course, been taken from them when they were captured.

These weapons were disposed as follows: Biggles took their own rifle and a dagger, Algy kept his automatic and the other dagger, while Ginger took the Tuareg rifle. Kadar, at his own request, was given the lance. This done, they set off in single file towards the oasis, taking care to keep under cover, and ten minutes saw them on the outer fringe of it but still some distance from the pool.

They now proceeded with as much speed as was compatible with the utmost caution, and a little while later Biggles called a halt while he went forward to reconnoitre. He was soon back at a run. 'Come on,' he cried exultantly. 'The coast is clear. I believe the whole lot of them have gone up to the village.'

'If they'll stay away long enough we might be able to grab the whole lot and get it back to the machine,' said Kadar eagerly, as they ran forward.

'They'd have to stay away the dickens of a long time,' returned Biggles. 'We should have to make several journeys. Our best plan is to hide the stuff and make sure of it; then, if they'll give us time, we could shift it farther away.'

The pool came into sight, and it looked as if Biggles was correct, for not a soul was there. In high spirits, they hurried round to the side where all the stores had been piled in one large dump; and, apart from the petrol, they saw many of the boxes that were their own property and had formed part of the load of their own ill-fated caravan.

There were several depressions in the sand, of various sizes, as is usual among sand dunes, and Biggles chose one near at hand, not far from the edge of the water; it was fairly deep, yet small in extent. Into this they at once began to pile the cans, Biggles putting them together in compact form while the others fetched them. He would, as he explained to Algy, have preferred a hole farther away, but the job would then have taken more time, and if the Tuareg returned before it was complete, then all their labour would be in vain.

It took them nearly half an hour to move all the cans, and Biggles was about to tell Kadar to bring one or two boxes to top up, when, to everyone's dismay, Algy's automatic cracked. A moment later he burst out of the trees, pale with alarm.

'I couldn't help it!' he cried. 'The devil nearly got me.'

'What are you talking about?' snapped Biggles.

'An Arab. He must have been left on guard, but went to the edge of the trees to watch the village. I ran slap into him, and I had to shoot because —'

'Never mind why,' broke in Biggles crisply. 'The damage is done. It couldn't be helped, but I am afraid the report will bring the others back. All hands to cover up the cans. Quick's the word.'

In a moment they were all pushing and kicking at the sides of the depression, flinging the sand over the precious tins. But the task was still incomplete when a shout came from the direction of the village.

'Don't stop,' panted Biggles. 'At all costs we must finish this; we've got to make the sand level. Kadar, get where you can see the track, and tell us when you see them coming.'

Kadar ran obediently to the top of a knoll, while the others continued their work at frenzied speed, but almost at once Kadar called a warning.

'They're coming!' he shouted.

Biggles did not stop what he was doing until the task was complete. Then he smoothed the top over to remove all signs of the cache, knowing that in a few moments the sun would dry the fresh sand to the colour of that around it. Satisfied at last that it could not be improved, he ran up the knoll to where Kadar was standing. The others followed, and thus they were all in a position to witness a startling and utterly unexpected change in the situation.

The Tuareg were pouring down the hill, some of them having begun a sort of enveloping movement. But they were no longer the only people in sight. From both sides of the hill, from the cacti, from the corn fields, and anything else that offered cover, came a crowd of amazing figures. They observed no military formation, but they were clearly soldiers, for they all wore a similar costume, or uniform – if a suit of armour can be called a uniform – and were equipped with one of two weapons: either a long-handled, moon-bladed battle-axe or a short curved sword, and a round, knob-studded shield.

For a moment Biggles could only stare spellbound at this amazing array, but Kadar was dancing with excitement. 'It's Cambyses' army,' he cried over and over again.

'Rot!' broke in Biggles tersely. 'People don't live for two thousand years.'

'Well, they are wearing the same armour and carrying the same weapons,' explained Kadar, somewhat abashed.

'So they may be, but I should say they are a lot of Arabs who have found the remains of Cambyses' army —'

'Arabs!' cried Kadar. 'They're not Arabs. They're white.'

Biggles stared again and saw that it was true. 'Never mind what colour they are, we had better bolt for it; we can't face that mob,' he muttered, and turned to run, only to throw up his hands despairingly as he saw another crowd, spread out in the form of a crescent, advancing from the other side and effectually cutting off their retreat. It was a perfect ambuscade. 'Well, this looks like being the end of the performance,' he observed bitterly. 'The only bright spot seems to be that Zarwan will get it in the neck as well. Here come the Tuareg; I must say they don't lack for courage.'

If the tribesmen had aimed to cut off the Tuareg from the oasis, and it looked as if that had been their intention, their scheme just failed, for although some of the Tuareg had fallen, the survivors, fighting fiercely with rifle and dagger, managed to break through; but then, seeing that Zarwan was in full flight towards the oasis, they broke and followed him. Upon this, the tribesmen let out a wild yell and charged.

Biggles folded his arms. 'Did you ever see such a sight in your life?' he murmured.

'Are you going to try to stop them?' cried Algy.

Biggles laughed shortly. 'Don't be silly; it would need a machine-gun company to do that. There is just a remote chance that if we can make them understand that the Tuareg are our enemies as well as theirs they may let us go, but I wouldn't like to bet on it. Still, if we start killing them we shall certainly seal our fate, so we shall be better advised to do nothing. There is one thing I am going to give myself the satisfaction of doing, though. Give me your pistol and take this rifle, Algy.' He thrust the weapon into Algy's hands, took the pistol, and then, as if changing his mind, he put it in his pocket and picked up a camel-wand – the yard-long cane used by all camel drivers.

Zarwan, green with terror under his brown skin, came bursting through the trees, imploring the airmen in broken English to protect him, although how he imagined that this could be done he did not say.

'Yes, I'll protect you, you murdering swine,' snarled Biggles, and before the others realized what he was going to do he had seized the abject half-caste by the back of the collar and began laying on the cane with all the power of his arm.

Two or three of the Tuareg dashed past, making for their camels; they took not the slightest notice of their leader's howls and screams. Nor did Biggles take any notice of the Tuareg, but continued laying on the cane, while the others watched the amazing spectacle, feeling that the villain was getting less than he deserved.

At last the camel-wand broke into halves; Biggles flung the pieces aside, and hurled the now sobbing half-caste from him. Then, with a curious expression on his face, as if he had suddenly remembered where he was, he looked about him. The others, following his example, saw that they stood in the centre of a ring of warriors, who had evidently stopped at the unusual exhibition they had discovered. A small party held three scowling Tuareg prisoners.

'Well,' said Biggles fatalistically, 'we shall soon know the verdict. Hello, look at this,' he went on quickly, as a tiny, monkey-like figure, waving a fly-switch made of the tail of some animal, came prancing through the ranks of the warriors. Suddenly it stopped dead and let out a series of piping shrieks in an unknown language.

Instantly, as if it was an order of some sort, the warriors closed in about the airmen, and holding them by the arms, started off up the hill towards the village.

'That's the creature we saw in the tombs, isn't it?' said Kadar.

Biggles nodded. 'Yes, I think it's the old lady herself,' he agreed.

CHAPTER 14

A HOPELESS PROSPECT

'SURELY this crowd couldn't have been in the village when we were up there?' said Algy, as they marched along.

'It's all a mystery to me,' declared Biggles. 'How they all managed to keep themselves hidden until the crucial moment is more than I can imagine.'

'It is my opinion that they were not in the village at all, but in some place beyond it, and the old hag went and fetched them,' announced Kadar.

'That may be the answer,' agreed Biggles, glancing over his shoulder. 'All the same, they must have been watching us for some time; anyway, they seem to realize that we are two parties, or I don't think they would keep us apart. Zarwan and the three Tuareg are following along behind, and they are being handled pretty roughly.'

'I wonder what these people are going to do with us,' said Kadar plaintively. 'I am sure that this is an unknown tribe, and that they are the descendants of Cambyses' army. How else could they get their white skins? At least, if they are not white, they are nearly white. They are certainly not Arabs.'

'I don't care two hoots about the colour of their skins,' muttered Biggles. 'It is the way they are likely to behave that matters. They can be Persians, Chinese, Eskimos, Red Indians, or anything else, as far as I am concerned, so long as

135

they don't try any funny tricks. They look a savage lot to me.'

'What else would you expect?' protested Kadar. 'If they are the descendants of people who came here thousands of years ago, and all that time have remained untouched by outside influences, it is only to be supposed that their habits will be the same as their forefathers', and they were – well, rather wild.'

'Well, we've found your missing oasis for you, so you won't mind my saying that the sooner I'm out of it the better I shall be pleased. In fact, I've got a feeling that before this business is over we shall be sorry that it didn't remain missing. Do you know anything about their language?'

'I couldn't speak it, but given time I might be able to write it. I shall try the experiment at the first opportunity.'

'All right; you go ahead with your notebook. By that time I hope I shall be on my way home,' answered Biggles.

They had now passed under the archway into the courtyard of the ants, but no halt was made. Instead, the procession proceeded down one of the streets on the near side and, after going for some distance, came to what looked like a moat, with sheer sides, some ten feet deep, cut out of the living rock. There was no water in it, but it was not empty. A drawbridge spanned it, and as they passed over they instinctively glanced down. A gasp of horror broke from Ginger's lips, and even Algy muttered something, for the entire bottom, as far as they could see, was a writhing tangle of snakes.

'Very pretty,' muttered Biggles in a hard voice. 'I fancy the object of that dyke is to keep the snakes on the right side of it, but quite a number fall in.'

'I shall never forget that sight as long as I live,' declared Algy. 'And I shall feel sick every time I think about it.'

'You'll have plenty of other things to think about in the near future, unless I'm mistaken,' Biggles told him grimly, as they were halted in front of a large, important-looking building with an iron-studded door – the first one they had seen. The door was opened, and they were urged inside.

After the glare outside they found it hard to see where they were, but their captors jostled them along, up a long winding flight of stairs, into a small room lighted by a single square window. The door slammed and they were alone.

'Well, at least we are together, and that's something to be thankful for,' muttered Biggles, as he crossed over to the window and looked out. 'Hello, I can see the oasis,' he went on. 'It looks as if we are in one of those high buildings perched on the wall; it must be a good seventy or eighty feet to the ground, which is a bit too far to drop, even if we could get through the window, which we can't, anyway, because it is too small.'

The room was absolutely destitute of furniture, so, thoroughly tired after their exhausting adventures, they squatted down on the dusty stone floor.

'We've been in some queer places in our time, but this trip has been about the limit,' snorted Ginger disgustedly. 'We've been out of the frying-pan into the fire ever since we started.'

'We're in the fire now, at all events,' agreed Biggles.

'What are we going to do about it?' inquired Algy.

'If you can think of anything I should be grateful, for I'm dashed if I can,' answered Biggles.

'But this is most interesting,' began Kadar, but Biggles cut him short.

'For goodness' sake stop guessing who these people are and where they came from,' he told him. 'You can spend the rest of your life guessing after we get home. For the present, try to think of something more helpful.'

'But did you see their shields?' asked Kadar eagerly.

Biggles shook his head sadly. 'I saw their faces, and that was enough for me,' he muttered. 'Whatever they have in store for us, you can bet your sweet life that it is not pleasant; if it is, then they have an odd way of welcoming strangers.'

'It is doubtful if they ever had any before,' returned Kadar.

'Nor, if it is left to me, will they ever have any more,' Biggles told him shortly. 'Well, I suppose we can only wait and hope for the best.'

The atmosphere of the little room was heavy, and they were all thankful when the light began to fade and the sun to lose its heat. The short twilight passed, and night fell.

'This is getting pretty monotonous,' grumbled Algy, standing up and staring out of the window, the window being merely a square hole left in the structure. He tried to get his shoulders through it, but, as Biggles had said, it was too small. He next turned his attention to the sides of it, to see if there were any possibility of its being enlarged, but his efforts were interrupted by the arrival of three warriors, who brought with them some water, dates, and a soft substance that looked like crushed maize mixed with water. One carried a small torch of palm fibres bound together.

Kadar tried speaking to them in several languages, but the warriors, who they now saw had a definite Eastern cast of features, only shook their heads. Just as they were about to leave, one of them, with something approaching a smile, pointed to the window, whereupon Kadar showed him something that he had written in his notebook. The man smiled more broadly, took the pencil which Kadar held in his hand, and made a series of marks in the book underneath what he had written; then, without waiting to see if what he had written was understood, he went out with the others.

'They are certainly Persians,' declared Kadar, who had gone across to the window to study the marks in the uncertain light of the stars.

'Never mind what nationality they are, what does that fellow say?' inquired Biggles quickly. 'Can you read it?'

Kadar shook his head. 'No,' he said, 'but the characters of two words might be broadly interpreted to mean "sacrifice" and "crocodile".'

Biggles started. 'I wouldn't translate any more of it if I were you,' he answered grimly. 'Those two words, used together, have a rather disconcerting significance.'

Kadar shrugged his shoulders. 'I can't make anything out of the rest of it, anyway,' he said, 'but judging by the signs that fellow made, I think he meant us to watch something through the window.'

'He may have meant that we could watch a sacrifice to the crocodile by looking through the window,' suggested Ginger.

'Well, that would be better than taking part in the show ourselves,' murmured Biggles, and a moment or two later it seemed that Ginger's supposition was correct, for, with a banging of cymbals and loud chanting, a torchlight procession emerged from the entrance to the village, which could just be seen, and started to wind its way down the hill. In front of it danced the unmistakable figure of the old hag.

'By gosh! It looks like Zarwan!' cried Ginger. 'I can't be sure because he is struggling, and the others keep getting in the way.'

Biggles pushed him aside. 'I think you're right,' he said, staring down at the eerie scene. 'I am not, I hope, vindictive, but even if they are taking him to the crocodile, and that is what it looks like, I shan't break my heart about it. After all, he arranged something even worse than that for us. But why aren't the Tuareg there, I wonder; I can't see them anywhere.'

'They are probably holding them for slaves,' offered Kadar. 'It is the customary treatment for prisoners in the desert.'

'Ah! That may be it,' murmured Biggles, who was still gazing through the window.

By this time the procession had reached the oasis – by crowding round the window they could all see it – and there was no longer any doubt but that the pool was its objective. The actual water could not be seen, but the waving torches were clearly visible and marked the head of the column. The chanting became wild, hysterical screaming. Then, with the abruptness of a wireless-set or a gramophone suddenly turned off, silence fell. But this did not persist for very long; it was broken by a sound which everyone in the room recognized at once, for they had all heard it before at one place or another. It was the coughing bellow of a crocodile.

Biggles turned away from the window, for apart from the torches little could be seen.

'I should say that human sacrifice to the crocodile is an ancient religious rite with these people, as it was with other desert tribes years ago,' observed Kadar quietly.

Biggles eyed him moodily. 'Whether it is a religious ceremony, or merely just fun and games, makes little difference to the poor devil flung into the pool,' he said thoughtfully. 'I ought to have shot that diabolical creature when I had the chance. Well, I've still got the pistol tucked into my armpit, so it may come to that yet. Before he gets his teeth into me that pretty little pet of theirs is going to have his tonsils tickled by as many bullets as I can plonk into them.'

As he finished speaking there arose a mighty shout from the pool; it ended in a frenzied singing, and presently Algy announced that the procession was starting back.

'Evidently the end of the first house,' remarked Biggles. 'It now remains to be seen if the performance is held twice nightly.'

For an hour they waited in breathless expectation, but they remained undisturbed. Silence had fallen, and at length Biggles turned to the food, which remained on the floor where the warriors had placed it.

'I've had better dinners than that put before me in my time, but we might as well make the best of it,' he observed.

Conversation flagged as they proceeded to eat all that there was to be eaten. This done, Biggles spent some time examining the window, and afterwards the door. Finally he joined the others where they were sitting on the ground with their backs against the wall. 'With a hammer and cold-chisel, and a few months to work in, we might make the window large enough to get through. Then, if we had a hundred feet of rope, we might get down,' he muttered sarcastically. 'But as we have none of these things I suppose we might as well try to get some sleep.'

Nobody answered. Ginger, worn out, was already dozing. Presently he slipped sideways so that his head rested on Biggles's leg. Biggles did not move. He took out his last remaining piece of cigarette from an inside pocket and puffed at it slowly while it lasted. Outside, the silence of the desert night remained unbroken.

CHAPTER 15

CONDEMNED TO THE CROCODILE

THE dawn came, and one by one the prisoners stretched their cramped limbs and sat up from the recumbent positions into which they had fallen; that is, all except Biggles, who was still sitting propped against the wall with his elbows on his knees and his chin cupped in the palms of his hands. It was some time before anyone spoke, for it seemed useless to talk of anything but their plight, and no one, it appeared, had any fresh observations to make on it. As Biggles had said, there was nothing they could do but wait.

Some time later they all looked up expectantly as, following a tramping of footsteps outside, the door was opened, and the same three warriors who had waited on them the previous evening brought in a further supply of the same unpalatable rations. They did not speak or make any signs; they simply set the food on the floor and went out again.

'How about trying to knock those fellows over the head the next time they come in?' suggested Algy.

'I have been thinking about the same thing,' answered Biggles. 'It is a difficult proposition. The trouble is, we don't know what they intend to do with us. For all we know, they may not intend to kill us, but if we set about these guards and manage to get out, and are afterwards taken again, we shall

142

have pretty short shrift. Another thing that must be considered is that drawbridge we came over. I have a feeling that the moat goes completely round this part of the village, otherwise there would be no point in having a bridge. That bridge is normally kept up, or it would not have been necessary to lower it to let us come across. Again, if all the people we saw yesterday are still about, and we can only assume that they are, we couldn't hope to fight our way through them, let down the bridge, and get out. In any case, even if we were successful in doing that they would probably catch us again, since they must know every inch of the ground and are no doubt faster on their feet than we are. It's a long way back to the machine, and when all is said and done, it wouldn't be much good going back to it empty-handed. They would overtake us there, if not before. Then there is the question of petrol. Even if we were lucky enough to get hold of a few cans, as many as we could carry, and get them back to the machine, what use would they be to us? We've got to get right back across the desert or it would be better not to start. A forced landing half-way, through shortage of fuel, would mean the end of us as certainly as any way these people could devise. It seems to me that there would be very little object in leaving the village for the hills, even if we could manage it, for we should simply be fugitives, and sooner or later they would be bound to recapture us – unless we died of thirst in the meantime.'

Algy nodded. 'Yes, it's the very dickens of a proposition, I must say,' he confessed. 'Yet this sitting here doing nothing is a bit nerve-trying.'

'Let us have some breakfast and forget about it,' suggested Biggles. 'Which will you have, Ginger, bacon and eggs, or a couple of nice grilled herrings? If you would prefer toast and marmalade, just say so.'

'I think I'll try a little porridge,' grinned Ginger, and

Biggles passed him the crushed maize, which was contained in a beaten copper vessel. No eating utensils had been provided, however, so it was necessary to scoop up the mess with the fingers.

They all ate as much as they needed, and then settled back in their original positions to pass the time.

The day seemed unending, for their captors did not reappear. However, all things come to an end, and at last the sun began to sink over the western hills.

'Suppose they try to repeat this crocodile stunt with us, what are you going to do?' Algy asked Biggles after a long silence.

'Just fight as hard as we can in the hope that they will club us over the head,' returned Biggles briefly.

Another silence fell, during which the sun set and a crescent moon appeared. Shortly afterwards a cymbal began beating not very far away, and presently footsteps were heard coming up the stairs outside.

'Here come the boys in the tin suits,' murmured Biggles, starting up. 'Now we shall soon know the worst, I fancy.'

Things turned out rather differently from what they had expected. For some reason or other, although they had not discussed it, the prisoners had taken it for granted that they would not be separated; that whatever fate was reserved for one would apply to all. This, up to a point, may have been correct, but it had not occurred to them that it might happen one at a time, so to speak. As it was, a large party of guards appeared; a smaller quantity of food and water was set upon the floor; but then two of the guards, instead of withdrawing, crossed the room, and, touching Biggles on the arms, made unmistakable signs that he was to follow them.

When he realized what was intended Algy sprang to his feet in a threatening attitude, as though he would have started the last fight then and there, rather than that they should be separated; but the point of a sword at his throat forced him back, impotent, against the wall.

'Don't give up hope,' Biggles told the others from the door. 'There is plenty of time for anything to happen. Watch the pool and you may see something.' He had no time to say more, for before he had finished speaking the escort was jostling him towards the door.

Now as he walked down the stairs he had one great fear, and that was that his hands would be tied together as a preliminary to the ceremony, if the crocodile sacrifice was, in fact, intended. This would make him utterly helpless, and he had decided in his mind that rather than allow it to happen he would produce the automatic, which he still carried under his arm, and make the best fight he could before he was killed, as would be bound to happen at the end.

However, to his infinite relief, no attempt was made to tie him, although this may have been due to some extent to his behaviour, for he obeyed instructions as meekly as a lamb. Or it may have been that the great crowd which surrounded him as soon as he was in the street made such a precaution, in the eyes of the warriors, quite unnecessary. Anyway, his hands were left free, and when the procession moved off he strolled along with them in his trousers' pockets as though he was merely out for an evening walk. In front gambolled the old hag. Behind her came torchbearers and then the cymbal beaters, the cymbals being, he now saw, two shields clashed together. More torchbearers and cymbal players fell in behind, while the rest, the spectators, brought up the rear.

In this fashion the procession advanced to the archway that formed the entrance to the village, where the hag began singing in her high reedy voice, occasionally darting back to lash Biggles across the legs with her fly-switch. The chant was taken up by everybody except Biggles, and it swelled louder and louder as the column wound its way slowly down the hill towards the pool.

A queer smile played about the corners of Biggles's mouth as the sheet of placid water came into view, and he saw its ghastly inmate standing on the edge, with its forefeet resting on the dry sand. Doubtless it knew all about the procession and its purpose, having been fed in this way for generations.

Slowly the procession drew nearer; the singing rose to a pitch of fanatical frenzy, and the leaders of the cavalcade began to open out so that a sort of semi-circle was formed, with Biggles standing alone in front of it. Before him was the water, and on the edge the waiting crocodile, with saliva dripping from the corners of its gaping mouth.

The semi-circle now began to advance, very slowly, so that it would presently force the victim into the jaws of the waiting crocodile, but what Biggles had hoped for had come to pass, and he was now acting in a very surprising manner. So surprising, in fact, that the chanting of the simple tribesmen began to lose its volume, and presently died away altogether. It may have been that no prisoner had ever before behaved in such an extraordinary way. Biggles did not know, nor did he care, as he carried on with his acting.

Raising his right arm towards the moon, he began singing in his rather unmelodious baritone, and the song he sang – the first one that came into his head – was 'Rule, Britannia'. It is doubtful if it had ever before been sung under such peculiar conditions, or in a more remarkable place. This thought actually occurred to him, and, in spite of his predicament, as he sang he wondered what on earth the others would be thinking, knowing that they would be able to hear him; and as he sang he edged slowly along, with the mincing steps of a ballet dancer, towards the right.

The faces of the spectators registered only astonishment and wonder. It was obvious that not for one moment did it occur to them that the prisoner might be about to attempt to escape; and for this there was some justification, for a solid semi-circle of armed warriors, a dozen deep, hemmed him in on all sides. Indeed, there seemed to be not the remotest possibility of escape.

But Biggles had now reached the spot for which he had been making, and, still singing with extraordinary vehemence, accompanied from time to time by a dramatic wave of his right arm, he dropped to his knees and began scraping at the surface of the sand, while the crowd, by this time overcome by curiosity, pressed nearer to see what he was doing.

A gasp went up as he dragged a can of petrol to the surface, and for a moment beat a tattoo upon it with the special key-opener that he had now taken from his pocket. He realized that the ignorant savages had not the remotest idea of what it was; nor was there any reason why they should, since it was unlikely that a can of petrol had ever before been within five hundred miles of the oasis. Judging by the hissing and muttering that went on, they took the whole thing as some sort of magical manifestation in which the moon played a part; at any rate, several of them glanced furtively towards it.

Six times Biggles repeated this performance, until six cans, three of them capless, stood on the sand beside him. The three with the caps intact he stood a little to one side, after which he scraped the sand back into the hole which he had made. Then, taking one of the open cans by the handle, he stood up, and with the other hand grasped it by the base.

There was a breathless hush while the crowd waited to see what was going to happen next.

Biggles did not keep his audience waiting. Raising the can high about his head, he swung it so that the spirit flew in all directions, but chiefly in front of the crowd. Naturally, quite a lot of it splashed on the feet of those in the front rank, and some may have gone on the people behind. Biggles did not care. Two cans he emptied thus, while the heavy stench of vapourizing petrol rose on the stagnant air. He was about to repeat the operation with the third can when some instinct of danger made him look round. To his horror he saw that the crocodile, evidently impatient, had come up out of the water, and was now rushing at him with open jaws.

The only thing he held in his hands which he could use as a weapon was the petrol-can, and this he flung straight into the creature's mouth, at the same time jumping back. He was only just in time. As it was, the crocodile's massive jaws came together, but instead of closing over the legs of its supposed victim, its yellow teeth sank into the thin metal tin as a fork goes into a ripe pear. The petrol at once gushed out through the holes, and apparently the beast did not like the taste of it, for it at once set up a hideous bellowing. This was answered by shouts from the crowd, and Biggles judged that the time had come for the grand finale of his performance.

The crocodile was standing about three yards away, shaking its great head as it strove in vain to rid itself of the unpalatable morsel. Very deliberately Biggles took his automatic from under his arm, and, taking careful aim, fired into the open jaws. A stream of sparks leapt from his hand to the crocodile's mouth.

Whatever he may have hoped for was far surpassed by what actually happened. Only those who have seen the contents of a two gallon petrol-can in flames can have any idea of what it is like. The crocodile was in the middle of one of its bellows; a sheet of flame shot out of its mouth so far that it actually scorched Biggles's legs. For a split second the reptile stood still, while sheets of flame spurted out of its mouth and poured back over its body where it had thrown the petrol. Then, with a frightful roar, it charged madly at the crowd.

Instantly all the loose petrol that Biggles had splashed about went up in a great sheet of flame, and the most appalling pandemonium ensued that it is possible to imagine. Flames were everywhere. The very air seemed to be on fire – as indeed it was, for it was saturated with petrol vapour. All those warriors who had been in the front rank rushed about screaming while they tried to extinguish their blazing legs, but they only flung the burning spirit on their companions who were behind. Into this incredible inferno, which reminded Biggles of nothing so much as an old print he had once seen of Hades, charged the crocodile, bellowing, blowing out streams of flame with each breath it took, and spraying blazing petrol over everything and everyone that crossed its path. It was, in very truth, the ancient conception of the dragon come to life.

Biggles himself was stunned. For a moment he could only stare, nearly as frightened as his wretched victims, while the reek of singeing hair filled his nostrils. His own eyebrows had gone, as had the front of his hair, but he did not realize it then. His legs were still smarting from the first blast of the crocodile's fiery breath.

The crowd had dispersed, although screaming fiery figures still tore wildly about among the palms; so, snatching up the three remaining cans of petrol, he tucked them under his left arm, and with his automatic ready for action in his right hand, he made off through the trees towards the hill that loomed darkly in the background, and the path that led to the tombs of the dead.

CHAPTER 16

BIGGLES WINS THROUGH

It was the old hag who saw him first, as he dodged from tree to tree towards his objective. Most of the warriors who had not actually fled from the spot were far too concerned with themselves to worry about anything but their burns, but a few who had got away unscathed began to rally to the old woman's urgent cries.

Biggles cursed her inwardly, for she began to appear as his evil spirit. He had hoped that no one would see which way he went, for this would enable him to get a long start, but the mummy-like female saw to it that in this he did not succeed.

He passed the crocodile, still writhing feebly in a pool of dancing blue flames, and it was clear that the brute was near to death, from which he derived considerable satisfaction. Whatever happened now, he thought, he had at least escaped the fate of being torn to pieces by the monster; but sounds of pursuit now reached his ears, although a quick glance over his shoulder revealed nothing, owing to the heavy shadow in which that part of the valley lay. He reached the bottom of the hill and found the narrow path, but already he realized what a handicap his burden of three full petrol-cans was likely to prove. However, he clung to them, determined to retain them as long as possible.

The night was hot, and the heat thrown off by the sun-drenched rocks caused perspiration to pour down his face, for there was no sun to dry it off as there was during the daytime. On he struggled, with the sounds of pursuit drawing ever nearer; above them rose the old hag's screeching. He reached the limit of the shadow, and as he broke into the moonlit area there was a wild yell behind him. But he did not stop longer than was necessary to change over one of the petrol-cans, for the arm under which he had been holding them was becoming numb with the strain.

About three-quarters of the way to the entrance to the tombs he took another glance over his shoulder and saw that about a score of warriors were on his trail, led by the hag, who was some distance in front. These twenty men would be more than he could conveniently manage, should they succeed in overtaking him, he thought desperately; yet he could go no faster without discarding his precious burden, and this he was not yet prepared to do, so he struggled on, drawing his breath in great gasps as the path became steeper towards the summit.

Fifty yards short of the entrance to the cave he realized that he would not be able to reach it, for his pursuers were less than that distance behind and were now fast overtaking him, due to some extent to their natural physical hardihood, and partly to the fact that they were unburdened. For a few more paces he staggered on, and then he turned at bay.

His pursuers were now coming through a narrow causeway between two high rocks, at a point where the path sloped up very steeply, and although he regretted it, he decided that he would have to abandon one of his cans, if only to leave a hand free for the automatic. Nevertheless, it was not his intention merely to leave it behind. Quickly unscrewing the cap, he hurled the can straight down the path into the faces of the leading tribesmen. Down the path it went, bouncing over the rocks and discharging its contents in all directions.

Then, taking out his matches, he struck one and tossed it into the track of his unusual missile.

A curtain of fire rushed along in the wake of the bouncing can, which had not yet quite reached the tribesmen. In the petrol-soaked air, the flames travelled as swiftly as a train of gunpowder, and overtook the can on the top of a bounce just in front of the warriors. For a moment, as it described a wide arc through the air, it presented an amazing spectacle, appearing as a comet dropping from the sky; then, with a roar, it exploded, shooting lines of fire in all directions like a bursting rocket.

Biggles waited for no more; hastily picking up the two remaining cans, he summoned all his strength and made a rush for the entrance to the cave, which he succeeded in reaching. For a moment he paused, staring down the hill behind him. His path was still marked by a line of curling blue flames, but of the tribesmen there was neither sight nor sound. Satisfied with his inspection, he started off along the cave.

Progress now became much slower, for several reasons, although the petrol cans were again the chief cause, for it was necessary to carry them both under one arm in order to leave the other free to hold a light. Again, he had very few pages left in his notebook, and it was essential that he should use them sparingly.

Unfortunately, his supply of matches was also running low, so he had to light one spill off another, and this resulted in a halt each time, while the petrol-cans were placed on the floor.

To make matters worse, he had an uneasy feeling that the hag, who he had good reason to suppose knew her way about the cave, might be following him, and although he did not fear her in the open, there was no knowing what devilment she might not practise in the eerie chamber. For this reason he often stopped to listen, but the only sound he heard was the occasional squeaking of a bat. Both matches and spills were exhausted before he reached the far end of the cave, having traversed the chamber of tombs without incident. With his last match, having no paper left, he lighted a strip of material torn from his shirt, but it burned badly, and in a short time went out, leaving him in the dark without further means of producing a light, so progress became both difficult and dangerous. Fortunately, as the cave was only a single passage, he had no cause to fear that he might become lost, so he continued on, feeling his way along the wall with his right hand, and holding the cans under the other arm.

He judged that it was nearly dawn by the time he approached the extremity of the passage, which he was able to identify by a rather sharp turning, and, remembering the scorpions, he dare not risk going on until it became light enough for him to see the exit. That last half-hour was perhaps the worst of all, for he could only sit still in the deathly silence knowing that without any means of making a light he was absolutely helpless should danger threaten. He derived some comfort from the automatic, which he again took out and held in his hand, but he did not need it, and at long last a vague grey light ahead told him that the new day was dawning.

In the interval of waiting, his thoughts had turned naturally to the precarious plight of the others. What would happen to them, after the appalling havoc he had caused at the pool, which included the death of the crocodile 'god', he dared hardly think. Still, it could not be otherwise, he reflected, for he certainly would not have helped them by allowing himself to be sacrificed. Nor did he know just what he was going to do when he reached the machine, assuming that he did. The petrol he carried, used economically, might keep the Tourer in the air for twenty minutes, not more. That would be time enough for him to fly the machine over to the oasis; but what then? The rest of the petrol was there, but would he be allowed to fill his tanks? It seemed hardly likely, unless the appearance of the strange monster out of the air terrorized the already shaken tribesmen. That was not too much to hope for, he decided, since it was reasonable to suppose that they had never before seen an aeroplane; anyway, therein lay his only chance, he thought, as he picked up the two cans and moved slowly towards the exit. With full tanks he might be able to help the others, but it was not easy to see how.

He was thankful to discover that there was no sign of the scorpions, so after a careful look round to make certain that all was clear, he went out, and started on the last lap of his journey.

A moment later he escaped death by an unpleasantly narrow margin when a boulder crashed down from the top of the precipice and buried itself, with a terrific thud, in the sand not half a dozen paces away from him. It so happened that it just touched a projecting piece of rock on the way down, and at the noise of the impact he turned in his tracks and threw a startled glance upwards. Seeing what was coming, he made a wild leap for safety, so that the missile, which he now saw was intended for him, missed its mark. Peering over the edge of the cliff was a tiny black head, and he knew at once to whom it belonged. The old woman, knowing that he had gone into the cave, and that he must ultimately emerge at one end or the other, had placed herself on the topmost part of the crag, from where she would be able to roll rocks down on him from whichever end he came out. So he reasoned as he proceeded to remove himself beyond the reach of further bombardment.

From a safe distance he turned and looked up, whereupon the old creature spat at him like an angry cat. Setting down the cans, he took out the automatic, but the hag evidently suspected its purpose, for she withdrew hurriedly; he watched the ridge for a minute or two, but when the head did not reappear he continued on his way, which by this time he knew quite well.

The sun was up by the time he reached the machine, which was still in the same position as it had been left, with the note he had written to Algy still pinned to the fuselage. There was some water inside the cabin, tepid, it is true, but he drank of it avidly, for his throat had become parched during the journey down the *wadi*. This done, he munched a few biscuits, and then set about preparing for what he suspected was likely to be his last flight.

There was not much to be done. The petrol he poured into the gravity tank, and then tossed the empty cans away. He removed the worst of the dust from the air intakes of the engines, and tested the controls, which he was relieved to find were in order. Sitting in the cockpit, he put a new clip of ammunition in his pistol, and satisfied himself that it was working properly; he also filled a pocket with spare clips from the box in the cabin. Finally, having loaded it, he placed the large-bore signal pistol on the seat beside him, and with it a dozen or so rounds of emergency signal-flares, red, green, and white, which the machine carried as part of its normal equipment.

Satisfied that there was nothing more he could do in the machine, he went down the *wadi*, removing from his proposed line of take-off the boulders, large and small, that lay in the way. A last look down the *wadi* and he returned to the machine, closed the door, and started the engines. He did not waste petrol in testing them for revolutions, or in warming them up, for the sun had already done that. Opening the throttle, he raced down the valley, leaving a swirling cloud of sand to mark his passage.

CHAPTER 17

A DREADFUL SENTENCE

GINGER never knew a more hopeless moment than when Biggles was led out of the room, for he never expected to see him again. The absence of his dominating personality and cheerful optimism made their own position seem so much worse; it was impossible to see how he could even hope to escape the fate designed for him by their captors. Algy, naturally, felt the same, and squatted down on the floor with his back resting against the wall in an attitude of utter dejection. Kadar, now that the blow had fallen, accepted the situation with oriental fatalism.

'It is the will of God; it will be as He decides,' he murmured, shrugging his shoulders, revealing the religious side of his nature for the first time; it was obvious that he was prepared to let it go at that. From his point of view, to attempt to divert the inscrutable ways of God, or even to wish otherwise, was a sin not to be contemplated, and he made no secret of it.

Neither Algy nor Ginger was inclined to argue about it, but had it been possible to do anything they would certainly have done it, for their experience indicated that it was unreasonable to expect God to help anyone who made no attempt to help himself. However, they did not discuss this difficult question, and as there was nothing they could do, they continued sitting on the floor in positions suggestive of acute misery.

'Has it struck anyone,' asked Ginger presently, 'what an extraordinary thing it is that, after being isolated for perhaps thousands of years, these people should have two lots of visitors from the outside world almost within a day of each other?'

'I think that it is not so much a coincidence as it may appear to be at first glance,' answered Kadar. 'I have been turning the matter over in my mind, and it is my belief that one was a direct cause of the other. In other words, had we not come here, Zarwan would not have come here either.'

'You mean you think he deliberately came here after us?' asked Algy.

'More or less. Actually, I think his intention was, in the first place, to prevent us from reaching here. I do not think for a moment that he ever came here himself before this occasion. An Arab, or Arabs, perhaps from Siwah, stumbled upon this place, and if that was so, they would certainly return to it, for such delightful watering-places are rare in this part of the world. Either on the first occasion, or later, they made contact with the people who live here, or perhaps with the old hag, and opened a sort of trade, bartering their wares after the fashion of Arabs with such things as the local people could offer.'

'You are thinking of the jewels?' put in Ginger shrewdly.

'That is precisely what I am thinking of. We know that the old woman is aware of the existence of the tombs, because that is where we discovered her; she may even be in the habit of visiting them regularly; in fact, she might even live there. No one can say how long the dead ones have been in that cave, and if I know anything about it, and I am not without experience, I feel quite sure that nothing would induce the

tribesmen to go into that death-chamber. There is another
necropolis just like it at Siwah, but no native would go near
it under any consideration. It is held to be haunted and not
without reason. But that old ghoul of a creature, if she did
not mind going into the place, as we have proved, would not
be beyond taking rings, necklaces, and other jewellery from
those who lie there. Even Arabs know the value of such things,
and those who came here probably exchanged such articles
as they had to offer for what the old woman found. They are
secretive by nature, so they would not talk about it; but in
due course the jewels would reach civilization, and it may
have been that Zarwan was the first man of importance to
see them. For all we know a regular traffic may have been
going on; indeed, I think it is more than likely. Don't you
see that that in itself would be a very good reason for Zarwan,
when he heard of my plans, to try to prevent me from getting
here? When he learned through his spies that I was trying to
charter an aeroplane, he decided to adopt more drastic
methods; as you yourselves saw, he was even prepared to
commit murder rather than that I should reach you. When
it was reported to him that you had agreed to fly me here,
he set off immediately with the Arabs who knew where the
place was in order to frustrate us. First, he ambushed the
caravan, which he realized would leave us stranded. After
that, no doubt he went on to the oasis which we had made
our headquarters in the hope of finding us there. Had he
succeeded, it is likely that we should now be drying in the
sun. But, owing to unforeseen circumstances, which may
have been very fortunate for us, we had already left, and
that must have put Zarwan in a quandary. Where were we?
Had we, after all, managed to reach the Lost Oasis? He decided to find out. Possibly he hoped, even if we were not here,
to do a profitable trade with the inhabitants, whom he doubtless imagined would be ordinary Arabs, or Bedouins of

some sort. If he thought that, then the reason why he kept the petrol is at once apparent; he intended to barter it as intoxicating liquor, to which all Arabs are prone, in return for jewels. Whether he fell out with the old woman, whether he tried to steal the jewels from her, or whether the old hag, alarmed by our intrusion, thought that he was trying to – how do you say? – double-cross her, we may never know. She went and fetched the tribe – unless, of course, some of them discovered us on their own account – with the result that we all know.'

Algy nodded approvingly when Kadar finished this rather long discourse. 'That all sounds reasonable to me,' he admitted. 'If the tribe treats visitors in this way it might well account for the fact that the oasis has remained undiscovered for so long. It would be interesting to know how many explorers have finished their travels in the crocodile's stomach.'

'I am convinced that these people are of Persian origin,' went on Kadar emphatically, lapsing into his old theme; but further conversation was checked by the noise of the procession as it emerged from the archway.

Ginger darted to the window. 'Great heaven!' he cried aghast. 'They're taking Biggles down to the pool. There he is, walking along just behind the front rank.'

Algy pushed him to one side in order to see. 'Yes, it's Biggles all right,' he muttered in tones of horror and despair. 'Why on earth doesn't he do something, I wonder? Surely he isn't just going to walk down to the pool and allow himself to be thrown in?'

'Not he,' declared Ginger. 'He's got some scheme in his mind, or he would not be strolling along as though he was going to somebody else's funeral instead of his own. I guessed he had something up his sleeve when he said "Watch the pool". That is where he will try to make a break. He'll give that crocodile a sore throat before it grabs him, I'll warrant.'

Nothing more was said for the moment. In breathless silence they all watched the torches approaching nearer and nearer to the dreaded pool; they could no longer see Biggles in person, but they could judge his position by the lights of the torchbearers. They heard the chanting rise to its highest pitch, and then die away suddenly.

'He's doing something,' muttered Ginger breathlessly. He was trembling with excitement.

Then arose in the still night air the most amazing sound ever heard in the Lost Oasis of Zenzura. There could be no mistake. It was Biggles singing 'Rule, Britannia'.

'Is he mad?' asked Kadar seriously, possibly thinking that the ordeal had driven Biggles out of his mind.

'Not so mad as some of those pig-faced Persians will be in a minute,' declared Ginger viciously. 'You wait till his gun starts popping.'

Then came a long delay, which was, of course, the period while Biggles was unearthing the petrol. But the watchers knew nothing about that; they had, in the stress of the moment, forgotten all about such things as petrol.

Suddenly there came a sound for which they had all been waiting – a single pistol-shot. But they were certainly not prepared for what followed, any more than the Persians were. The entire oasis in the region of the pool seemed to burst into flame, while into the night rose an outburst of yells and groans. Thereafter pandemonium broke loose.

'It's the petrol!' yelled Algy, beating on the window-sill with his fists in his excitement. 'It's the petrol! He's blown the whole perishing party up.'

'Attaboy! Attaboy! Set 'em alight!' screamed Kadar, lapsing suddenly and unexpectedly into American, which he must have picked up at some time or other from a western visitor.

'Gosh! I hope he hasn't blown himself up with it,' breathed Algy with a sudden change of tone, as the possibility of this occurred to him. Indeed, judging by the flames, it did not seem at all unlikely.

'The crocodile! Look at the crocodile!' cried Ginger tersely, as the beast charged through the trees, like a medieval dragon, breathing fire.

'Am I dreaming, or is this really happening?' asked Algy in a curious voice. 'It doesn't seem possible.'

'It doesn't, but it is,' declared Ginger enigmatically. 'I hope he's got away. I wish I knew.'

'Where the dickens will he go even if he manages to get clear?' demanded Algy. 'He said himself that there was no-where —'

'Anywhere would be better than down that brute's throat,' declared Ginger. 'If only he has got clear, anything can happen. Look at what he has done already. No one would have given a fig for his chance as he walked down there surrounded by that mob, yet he has sprung a surprise that not even we thought of – Great goodness! What's that?'

'It is a volcano,' declared Kadar, while they all stared at the blazing can of petrol which Biggles had just flung down the hill-side into the faces of his pursuers, 'It may be the end of the world,' he added thoughtfully.

'Not on your life it isn't,' said Algy crisply. 'It's petrol. He has got away and taken some petrol with him. You can see where he is. He has bolted up the hill and he has nearly reached the mouth of the cave. The crowd is after him, and he is bombing them with petrol-cans. Oh, lovely! Lovely! Frizzle, you blighters, frizzle!'

Nothing else happened, for, as we know, Biggles had gone into the cave. Presently the watchers suspected it, and although they remained staring through the window, the excitement eased somewhat.

'Well, would you believe that?' said Ginger at last. 'I honestly believe he has got clean away.'

'And what is going to happen to him now?' asked Algy soberly.

'And what is going to happen to us?' muttered Kadar nervously.

'It isn't much use guessing,' opined Ginger. 'As Biggles himself would say, we shall have to wait and see, but I must say that it has put new life into me to know that he has got away. I never felt so absolutely hopeless in my life as when I saw him going down the hill.'

'Some of the people are coming back, judging by the sound of it,' observed Algy. 'I can hear them groaning. It also sounds as if some of them are cursing, and I don't wonder at it, for a lot of them must have got pretty badly burned.'

'So shall we be, I'm afraid, when they remember that we are up here,' murmured Kadar pessimistically.

'Biggles won't overlook that possibility,' declared Ginger confidently. 'He'll see us through. While he is at large anything can happen.'

'I should like to know what these Persian johnnies are thinking about the whole thing,' muttered Algy.

'They are probably having a council to decide what shall be done with us,' suggested Kadar. 'Having had a taste of our magic, as they will suppose Biggles's effort to be, they'll think very carefully before they try any more sacrifices.'

'They may take the view that if one of us can kill their god by producing fire out of the sand, what might three be able to do?' said Ginger hopefully.

'I hope you're right,' declared Algy fervently.

After that they fell silent, and the night wore on. None of them slept, for in their extreme peril repose was out of the question. Never to any of them had a night seemed so long. Once or twice, when one of them thought he heard a sound below, he went eagerly to the window and looked down, thinking perhaps Biggles had returned, but on each occasion the alarm proved false.

At last the sky began to grey with the approach of dawn, and Algy yawned. 'My goodness! I'd give something for a hot bath,' he muttered. 'Never in my life have I felt so filthy. Hark! Is that someone coming?' he concluded sharply.

A moment later footsteps could be heard coming up the stairs, accompanied by the low mutter of voices. The door was thrown open and several bearded warriors, evidently leaders of the tribe, stood on the threshold, regarding the prisoners with scowling faces. It was not difficult to guess the reason for their displeasure, for nearly all of them showed signs of the recent conflagration. One had a terrible blister on his cheek, and another had had most of his beard singed off. In their hands they carried strips of hide, evidently to be used as bonds, suggesting that they were not going to risk a repetition of Biggles's moonlight magic.

'I don't like the look of this,' said Algy quietly.

Before either of the others could answer, even if they had so wished, the tribesmen came into the room, and without any more ado proceeded to tie their prisoners hand and foot. Algy and Ginger, as soon as they realized what was intended, attempted to put up a fight, but against such hopeless odds their efforts were doomed to failure from the onset. They were thrown roughly to the ground, and held securely while the thongs were adjusted. This done, they were hauled to the door like tailor's dummies being taken from a shop-window, and dragged down the stairs into the street, where a number of spear-armed warriors were waiting.

'Can you make a guess as to what they are going to do with us?' Ginger asked Kadar, for their heads were close together.

'No, but doubtless they have decided on an unpleasant way of killing us,' answered Kadar resignedly, and with that the assembly began to move off.

It was only with difficulty that they could see where they were being carried. Ginger went cold all over in spite of the heat as they crossed the drawbridge, for he had not forgotten the snakes underneath; but he breathed again as the procession moved on, and presently passed under the entrance arch into a world now flushed with the pink-and-gold of dawn. Presently the sun would mount above the hill-tops, and it would be baking hot, but Algy was doubting whether they would live long enough to feel its heat.

The procession passed along the side of the oasis, and as it reached the open space between the palms and the foot of the necropolis hill without showing signs of halting, Algy wondered where they could be going, for the leaders were still advancing towards the track that led to the tombs of the dead.

It was Kadar who told them the grim truth, and he had obtained the information in an unexpected manner. To his great surprise, a guttural voice near him whispered his name; turning his head with difficulty, he saw the Tuareg marching beside him with their arms bound securely to their sides, and he realized for the first time that the tribesmen evidently intended to dispose of all their prisoners at once. The faces of the Tuareg, gallant enough in battle, were a ghastly colour; their eyes rolled, and the teeth of one of them chattered in his head.

'What did you say?' Kadar asked the Tuareg who had spoken, in his own language, for he had not quite caught all the words.

'They are taking us to the tombs of the dead, to be buried alive,' answered the Tuareg hoarsely, and Kadar passed the information on to the others.

Ginger looked up at the blue sky which presently he would see no more, for already the procession had reached the foot of the hill. As he stared upwards a small black object soared into view; at first he thought it was a vulture, but when, a moment later, he heard the deep hum of the Tourer's engines, he understood.

The tribesmen heard the noise too, and the procession stopped, while a nervous mutter ran down the line.

'It's Biggles!' yelled Algy.

CHAPTER 18

BIGGLES STRIKES

AFTER taking off, Biggles had climbed swiftly to five thousand feet, and then, cutting his engines, began gliding towards the oasis, with his side window open, staring at the ground between the village and the foot of the hill.

In doing this he was following the plan he had decided to adopt. Not that he had much choice. He had enough petrol left in his tank for, roughly, five minutes' flying; at the end of that time he would have to come down wherever he was, and the only place that he could remember, apart from the *wadi*, where a landing might be made without disastrous results, was the open area between the palms and the foot of the necropolis hill. It so happened that his roving eyes had instinctively noted this piece of ground when they had walked across it, for it becomes second nature to most airmen to mark down a possible landing-ground when one is noticed. Biggles could not recall just what the surface of the ground was like, although he could not remember any serious obstructions; there were, he thought, a number of small pieces of loose rock, but none large enough to upset him. He did not relish the idea of landing there, but there was nowhere else. In any case, he could not get back to the *wadi* even if he had wished to – not that there would be any point in returning to the place which he had left only a few minutes

166

before. The petrol-supply was near the pool, and since he could not hope to carry the petrol to the machine, the machine would have to be taken to the petrol, whatever the risk.

He had not expected to see anyone there; he had hoped that after the débâcle of the previous night the place would be deserted, and a great wave of disappointment swept over him when he observed that, far from this being the case, a column of tribesmen was actually on the march across it. From the altitude at which he was flying he could not, of course, distinguish individuals, and although he noticed vaguely that the tribesmen were carrying something, it did not occur to him that it might be Algy and the others. Not unnaturally, he imagined that they were still in the place where he had left them, and he cast several glances in that direction, wondering if they could see him, and if so, what they were thinking at the reappearance of the machine in the air.

His petrol was now nearly exhausted; willy-nilly, a landing would soon have to be made, so he resolved forthwith to fall back upon his last forlorn hope, which was that the machine would put the natives to flight and give him an opportunity of getting more petrol – at least some of it, if not all. Beyond that he did not think, for the hazards of the undertaking were such that further arrangements were uncalled for; time would come for that if he was successful.

He had dived many machines in his time, both in peace and war, but never before had he dived one so recklessly as he dived the Tourer, for on no previous occasion had the circumstances been so desperate. With the engines full on he pushed the joystick right forward and held it there with his right hand, while with his left he picked up the signalling pistol, the modern equivalent of the war-time Very pistol. Down went the nose of the Tourer, while the tail cocked high into the air behind it. The roar of the engines became a pulsating bellow; the wind screamed through the wires and struts, while the quivering needle of the air-speed indicator crept round the dial – 200 – 300 – 350.

At just under four hundred miles an hour Biggles began to ease the stick back, for he was getting low, and he had no desire either to dive into the ground or end matters by stripping the wings off his machine; in any case, he saw that further speed was unnecessary, for already the tribesmen were scattering like chips from a log under a woodcutter's axe. At a hundred feet, with the engines still running on full throttle, he levelled out, his eyes running swiftly over the scene below, on the lookout for a suitable mark at which to discharge the pistol. He chose his target, and a ball of crimson fire went screaming down into the middle of a group of warriors; and it was at that moment that Algy's white face caught his eye. So astounded was he that he stared at it for a full second, forgetting for the moment that an aeroplane travels far in that time. He snatched the stick back, and his wheels missed the palms by inches. The manoeuvre served this good purpose, however: it turned the retreat of the tribesmen into a panic-stricken rout. Some fled helter-skelter, flinging away their weapons; others flung themselves flat and covered their faces with their hands.

If Biggles had been prepared to 'shoot up' the district before seeing Algy and the others, their unexpected appearance put a new zest into his actions, and he treated the savages, did they but know it, to as fine an exhibition of crazy-flying as has ever been seen at a flying-display. Round and round he tore, diving and zooming, with sometimes his wheels and sometimes a wing-tip nearly scraping the ground. On the brief occasions when he flew level he reloaded the pistol, holding the joystick between his knees, and blazed red and green fire at the now widely scattered natives. Few were, in fact, still in sight, and these he chased until their actions became ludicrous. One dropped to his knees and raised his arms in an attitude of prayer.

Biggles was in the middle of a turn when his engines coughed, choked, and then cut out dead. Instantly the natives were forgotten as he concentrated absolutely on the tricky business of putting the machine down without damaging it. Never before had so much depended on a good landing, and he put all his skill into it. A gentle side-slip to the left brought him in line with the open area, with the nose of the machine pointing in the direction in which Algy and the others were lying. As he flattened out he wondered why they did not get up and run towards him, for his speed had not permitted him to see that they were tied; but now, as he skimmed low over them, he understood.

Slowly the machine sank nearer to the sand, while his eyes stared at the track along which he must now land. One boulder would be all that was necessary to seal their fate, but, as it happened, although there were several small pieces of rock which caused the machine to bump and wobble dangerously, there was nothing large enough to throw it over, and it ran to a standstill, with stationary propellers, in an unaccustomed silence.

The instant the machine stopped running Biggles was out, racing back to where the others were lying. Once he paused to snatch a sword from the hand of a warrior who had either been hit by one of his shots, or had died of fright; then he went on again, and, panting, presently dropped on his knees at Algy's side.

'Are you hurt?' was all he said, as he cut him free.

'No,' answered Algy.

'Then take this pistol and run for the petrol,' ordered Biggles. 'Don't stop for anything. If anyone tries to get in your way, plug him. The petrol is our only chance.'

Algy ran off towards the trees, working his arms to restore the circulation.

Biggles cut Ginger's bonds, and told him to follow Algy. Then he freed Kadar, dragged him to his feet, and set off after the others. Not a soul attempted to stop them, and by the time he reached the *cache* the top cans were already uncovered. He snatched up two of them, and with a crisp 'Get 'em all out if you can manage it,' he raced back to the machine.

It took him two or three minutes to empty the two cans into the gravity tank, but it was time well employed. Into the cabin he darted, and without bothering to close the door, he started the engines and taxied swiftly but carefully to the edge of the trees, where he switched off and jumped out.

'Take this and mount guard,' he told Kadar tersely, thrusting into his hands the signal-pistol, in which a cartridge remained. 'If you see anyone coming, let drive. Ginger, get to the machine, and fill the tanks as we pass the cans to you. Take a couple with you.'

Perhaps never before in the history of aviation has an aeroplane been refuelled with such frantic haste. On one side of it a great pile of empty cans lay where they fell, as Ginger flung them aside after emptying them of their contents. Panting and staggering under the weight of the loads they carried, Biggles and Algy fed him with full ones, and not until only a few cans remained did he ease the pace.

'We are safe!' cried Biggles exultantly. 'We've done it! Keep your eyes skinned, Kadar. Don't let them surprise us.'

'I can see a few of them coming back in the distance,' called Kadar.

'Let us know if they get close,' replied Biggles, and went on with the work of refuelling until the last can had been emptied.

'Have we got enough to get us home, do you think?' panted Algy.

'I think so, but it is impossible to be absolutely certain,' answered Biggles. 'We've a long way to go. It's no use going merely to Semphis. It has got to be either Siwah or Dakhel. I fancy Siwah is our nearest contact-point with civilization, but not knowing just where we are, it's impossible to be sure. We can only take a course to the north-west, hoping to strike it. If we miss it we ought to be able to pick up a caravan, or a caravan trail, since we shall be in a district where people are moving about.'

When he had finished speaking Biggles took two spare water-bottles from the cabin and, running to the pool, filled them, a faint smile flitting across his face as he saw in daylight the scene of his adventure the previous night. Returning, he pointed out the dead, scorched body of the crocodile, still lying where he had last seen it. 'I warmed that beauty's tonsils for him, as I said I would,' he smiled. 'Hello, what's that – over there?' He pointed to a small dark object that lay at the foot of some rocks near the bottom of the hill.

'Great Scott! I believe it's the old hag!' cried Algy. 'Yes, by all that's wonderful, so it is. She must have tumbled down the rocks and broken her neck when you dived on the crowd just now – unless she died of fright.'

'Stay here and keep your eyes skinned, Ginger,' ordered Biggles. 'Yell if you see anyone coming.'

'Ay, ay, sir,' answered Ginger cheerfully.

Biggles, with Algy beside him, hurried across to the body, and they saw that it was indeed the old hag. A glance told them that she was stone dead, and a jagged wound in her forehead, which looked as though it had been caused by a fall, showed how she had at last met her death. She was a dreadful-looking creature, little more than a collection of bones covered by brown, wrinkled skin, and Biggles was about to turn away when Algy caught him by the arm.

'What are those things?' he asked, pointing to a little steam of what looked like semi-transparent marbles, some green and some red, that had evidently fallen out of a small goat-skin bag attached to the old woman's girdle.

Biggles picked one up, one of the red ones. 'Great heaven!' he whispered in an awed voice. 'I wouldn't swear to it, but I believe it's a ruby.'

'Look out, they're coming!' came Ginger's voice from the machine.

Biggles stooped swiftly, and jerking off the bag with a single tug, thrust it into his pocket, while Algy scooped up the loose stones. Then they turned and ran back to the others, hastened by shrill cries from the heart of the oasis, which suggested that the tribesmen were rallying there.

'All aboard,' cried Biggles, climbing into the cockpit. 'They'll change their minds about coming nearer, I fancy, when the engines open up.' He felt for the self-starter, and as the others scrambled aboard the powerful engines sprang to life.

Biggles taxied slowly to the extremity of the open area. Then, with his engines idling, he looked over his shoulder at Kadar. 'This Lost Oasis that you were so anxious to find,' he said, 'would you like to stay here and do a bit more exploring, or would you rather come home with us?'

Kadar smiled wanly. 'I think I've seen enough of it to last me for a little while,' he said.

'And I've seen enough of it to last me for the rest of my life,' Biggles told him definitely. 'Go steady with the water in there; there's a lot of sand between here and the place we are making for,' he added, and he eased the throttle forward.

The engines roared and the machine began to move

forward; the tail lifted; the wheels bumped gently once or twice, and then the Tourer soared into the air.

Biggles glanced at Algy as he levelled out and swung the nose of the machine round towards the north-west. 'It's queer how things turn out, isn't it?' he mused. 'Twenty-four hours ago, what we are doing now seemed as unattainable as the moon. It just shows that you never know. All I ask now is that the gees-gees in the engines go on kicking until we get to the other side of this confounded sand.'

'What a treat it will be to get a bath,' murmured Algy, as he settled down in his seat for the long flight ahead.

'I'll believe that there are such things when I see one,' returned Biggles, as his eyes went to the compass and then down to the sterile landscape underneath. The *wadi* in which they had first landed was slipping away below, and he knew that whatever happened he would never see the Lost Oasis of Zenzura again.

CHAPTER 19

MIRAGE!

For three long hours the machine roared on over the seemingly endless sand. To Ginger, sitting in one of the back seats, each passing hour, with nothing but dunes, and still more dunes, creeping up over the horizon, seemed more incredible than the last. It was hard to believe that such a place could exist on the face of a world that is assumed to be civilized and sophisticated. But here was nature as it always had been, and might be for ever.

To Biggles the period was one of intense strain. Before he had experienced real thirst he had not been particularly concerned at the prospect of flying over long stretches of open desert, but now that he knew the horror of it he could only sit with his eyes fixed on the horizon, inwardly praying that some speck, some living thing, even if it were only an isolated palm, would come into view to break the eternal monotony of the yellow waste. No ocean crossing he had ever made, and he had made many, had filled him with so much dread.

From time to time his eyes dropped for an instant to the fast-sinking petrol-gauge, only to return again to the horizon, while he tried to keep the machine as steady as possible in the heat-rocked atmosphere through which it bored. He realized more clearly than ever before what a tangible thing the atmosphere was; over the rolling dunes, some of them many miles in length, the air seemed as fluid as water and as unstable as a storm-tossed ocean.

'Something ought to show up soon,' murmured Algy at last, holding his shirt away from his body for relief, for the heat in the little cabin was appalling.

'Yes,' was Biggles's only answer.

'How much juice have we got left?'

'With the gravity tank, I reckon about forty minutes.'

Algy said no more, but, like Biggles, concentrated on the horizon. Never did shipwrecked sailor watch for land with greater anxiety.

Twenty-five minutes went past; it seemed like an hour, and still there was no sign of a break in the sand.

'It begins to look as though the whole blessed earth has turned to sand,' muttered Algy.

Biggles said nothing, but switched over to the gravity tank as the main tank petered out.

'Land ho!' cried Ginger suddenly.

Biggles started. 'Where away?'

Ginger pointed due north.

It was difficult to see anything clearly on account of the quivering haze, for now that the sun had nearly reached its zenith the air rocked and shook like a jelly, but by focusing his eyes on the spot indicated Biggles could just make out a faint blue smudge.

'Mirage,' said Kadar, softly.

'I hope you are wrong,' muttered Biggles. 'If that is what it is, then we are out of luck, but I think I can make out what looks like the top of some palms.'

Kadar was standing up, bent forward, peering through the windscreen in his anxiety. 'I am afraid of it,' he said. 'The curse of the desert is that you cannot trust your eyes. They often show you things that are not there. The things are, of course, somewhere, but what appears to be just in front of you can be fifty miles away in any direction. It is an illusion, simply a reflection on the hot atmosphere.'

'Hey! Look at that!' cried Ginger, pointing to a line of huge, distorted camels, their supercilious faces held high, marching along below.

Algy gave a shout of joy. 'A caravan,' he said.

Kadar shook his head. 'It is a mirage. I have seen too many not to recognize one when I see it. Watch, and see what happens.'

As the machine roared on the camels seemed to grow enormous, until they towered up far into the sky, an un-believable spectacle. Then they began to fade into the haze. More and more indistinct they grew, until, when the Tourer roared over the spot where they had been, there was nothing as far as the eye could see but sand; no longer wind-blown dunes, but a flat, gently undulating plain.

'See! They have gone,' said Kadar seriously. 'That is the usual way with a mirage. How many unfortunate people have seen visions of water, limpid streams, waving palms —'

'All right, don't make a song about it,' interrupted Biggles irritably. He was staring forward at the smudge, which had now become a dark, filmy green.

'I can see palms,' declared Algy.

'As likely as not you will see water presently,' returned Kadar quietly, 'but that does not mean that it is there. Do not think me pessimistic, but we must face facts, and a mirage is anything but a fact. It is pure hallucination.'

Biggles, still watching, saw the crest of a long line of palms appear; they seemed to grow rapidly larger, but at the same time there was something odd about them. Then he under-stood. They were upside-down, their fronds resting on the sand and their long straight boles pointing upwards to the sky.

Biggles blinked and shook his head. Then he looked again. 'Am I going crazy, or are my eyes going cock-eyed?' he snapped.

'Neither,' replied Kadar calmly. 'It is merely another trick of the mirage.'

'But do you mean to say that those things are not there?' demanded Algy incredulously.

'They are somewhere, or we should not see the reflection of them,' agreed Kadar, 'but they might be some distance away. They might even be below the skyline. Still, it is comforting to know that we are at least in the region of an oasis, and a caravan; but, as I have warned you, one cannot rely on them being where they appear to be. Look! Look! Now perhaps you will believe me.'

While he had been speaking the palms had suddenly assumed colossal proportions. They seemed to fill half the sky, and were all the more terrifying on account of the fact that they were still upside-down. Then, suddenly, for no apparent reason, they became a vague blur, and soon, like a cloud of smoke on a windy day, finally disappeared altogether.

'Heavens, what a country to live in,' groaned Biggles. He still held on the same course, for there appeared to be no point in altering it.

'How much petrol have we left?' asked Ginger.

'I wish you wouldn't keep asking that,' answered Biggles coldly. 'Ten minutes at the outside.'

Nothing more was said while the seconds ticked past on the watch on the instrument-board, and the sky turned from dull blue to an intense steely grey.

'Is that another storm coming?' asked Ginger.

'If it is, we're sunk,' said Biggles curtly. He was feeling the strain.

'I do not think so; the sky plays all sorts of tricks in such heat as this,' Kadar told them. He was now the chief spokesman, for his experience of desert travel could not be ignored.

'How far is it to the horizon?' asked Biggles. 'I ask because we shall not get to it – anyway, not in this machine.'

'How far would you think?'

Biggles frowned. 'I'm dashed if I know,' he said. 'I am not sure whether I am looking at it or not, and that's a fact. In normal conditions I should say fifty miles, since there appears to be nothing in the way to interrupt the view. One can see as far as that on a fine day in England, sometimes farther.'

Kadar regarded the skyline steadily for some seconds. 'It might be ten miles,' he said at last. 'It is certainly not more; it might be less.'

'But that sounds ridiculous,' argued Biggles.

'No doubt it does. In England you get fogs which restrict visibility. Here we get heat-haze which distorts everything hopelessly.'

'I'll take your word for it,' Biggles told him moodily.

'Look there!' shouted Ginger suddenly, pointing forwards and downwards, and the others stared in surprise as a long line of camels, each animal accompanied by its own dense black shadow, appeared in a manner which could only be regarded as miraculous, so close were they.

'Where the dickens did they come from?' ejaculated Biggles. 'I could have sworn a moment ago that there wasn't a living thing in sight. I suppose it isn't another mirage?' he concluded doubtfully.

'Oh, no,' declared Kadar definitely. 'That is the real thing. There is no doubt about it. Look how clear-cut everything is. There must have been a change in atmospheric conditions. It was the reflection of this caravan that we saw just now; it has appeared out of the invisible haze I told you about. The drivers have seen us.'

This was obviously true, for the line of camels had halted, and white-robed figures could be seen staring upwards.

Biggles was now in a quandary, for if they went on without finding the oasis they might lose the caravan; on the other hand, if they went down it might be only to learn that the oasis they were trying to reach was not far away. But if the sand was soft, as seemed highly probable, they would not be able to get the machine off the ground again. Should he go down, or should he risk going on?

Kadar seemed to guess what was going on in his mind, for he urged him to continue. 'If the caravan was so close, it is likely that the oasis is close, too,' he said.

A moment later his assumption was confirmed in a startling manner. The atmosphere seemed suddenly to clarify, and there, only a few miles away, was an unmistakable oasis.

'Siwah!' cried Kadar delightedly. 'I recognize it. Look, there are the ruins of Jupiter Ammon, the place Cambyses' army was trying to reach when it was overwhelmed. Is it not remarkable to think that for thousands of years the descendants of those same people have gone on living, while the temple their ancestors set out to plunder has been slowly falling into decay? They might have been a million miles away for all the hope they had of reaching it.'

Algy and Ginger looked with interest at the ancient ruins of such romantic association, but Biggles was more concerned with the present. He had already throttled back as far as he dared, to conserve his fast-diminishing supply of petrol, but he was still some distance away when, after the usual warning from the engines, it gave out, and he was compelled to put the Tourer into a glide. He had, however, nearly three thousand feet of altitude, and as the machine, with empty tanks, could glide for a mile to every thousand feet of height, he was able to reach the nearest palms with a hundred feet to spare.

Choosing the smoothest area he could see, he glided down to land.

In this landing, apart from the care he exercised, he may have been lucky, for had he gone on a little farther he would have struck a patch of soft sand, and the machine might have somersaulted with serious, if not fatal, results. As it was, it ran for a little way over fairly hard gravel before reaching the sand, so that by the time it did reach it its speed was greatly reduced. The machine shuddered and the tail cocked high as the clogging sand embraced the wheels; but it also acted as a brake, and although the machine stopped dangerously quickly, it did not turn over.

Biggles sank up to the ankles as he jumped down, and when the others joined him he pointed to the wheels, buried for half their depth in fine dust. 'We are lucky we are where we are,' he said grimly, 'for we should never get off this without help. You have been to Siwah before, Kadar; do you think there will be any difficulty in getting labourers to drag the machine clear of this stuff?'

'I do not think so,' answered Kadar. 'Money will do most things even in the desert, as it does in civilized places.'

Hardly had he finished speaking when, with a shout, a party of horsemen appeared from the direction of the village, riding at breakneck speed.

'What's the idea, I wonder?' asked Biggles anxiously. 'Do they mean trouble?'

Kadar was watching the horsemen with a perplexed expression on his face. 'I trust not,' he said. 'I don't see why they should —' He broke off, peering forward with an expression of astonishment. 'Why – why – it's Sarapion,' he cried.

'*Who*?' inquired Biggles.

'Sarapion. He is one of our servants,' explained Kadar in great excitement, and rushing forward, he embraced a white-clad Egyptian who slid gracefully from his horse.

They spoke together for a little while, and then Kadar returned to the others, his face beaming. 'My father is here,' he said joyfully.

'Good! That should make things easier for us,' smiled Biggles. 'But he was soon on our track, wasn't he?'

'Yes, but it came about like this. One of the men with our caravan was mounted on a very fast camel, and he managed to escape the massacre. By good fortune and great endurance he reached Siwah, and from there sent a message to my father to tell him what had happened. My father, may heaven preserve him, went at once to the Governor and asked for his assistance, and I believe he is about to send aeroplanes in search of us.'

'They would have been a long time finding us at Zenzura, I am afraid,' murmured Biggles doubtfully.

'Yes, but that does not matter now. My father came on to Siwah at once in a small aeroplane which he was able to charter, in the hope of arranging for caravans to go and search for us in the desert. By offering a big reward he was able to do this, and several Arabs have already left. No doubt it was one of the search-parties that we saw just now.'

'This is all very comforting,' declared Biggles. 'What had we better do now?'

'We shall have to stay here for a little while, I am afraid, while a messenger goes back to Mersa Matruh aerodrome and arranges for petrol to be sent out to us – unless, of course, you prefer to go back on a camel.'

'Not for me, thank you,' replied Biggles quickly. 'I'd rather ride an aeroplane than a camel any day. How are they off for water here?'

'Oh, there is plenty of water. There are even some lakes.'

'Lead me to one,' murmured Biggles. 'Tell me when we get to it, because I may have forgotten what a lot of water in one piece looks like.'

CHAPTER 20

FAREWELL TO THE DESERT

Two hours later, having bathed, shaved, and changed their clothes, they sat contentedly in a shady tent which had been pitched among the palms, telling Kadar's father the amazing story of their adventures.

The old man also had some news for them, which cleared up a lot of points, although certain of these were already suspected.

It appeared that the Society for the Preservation of Antiquities, the organization of which Kadar had told them, had been on Zarwan's trail for some time, although the members had raised no objection to Kadar's trip because his genuine and impersonal motives were well known. Zarwan had, in some way, got wind of this and bolted from Egypt, which accounted for his sudden disappearance while the airmen were making their preparations. Active members of the society had gone both to Khargah and Siwah to await his return, so even if he had escaped his fate at the hands of the lost tribesmen, it was likely that he would have found death waiting for him in his own country. Moreover, the Egyptian police were on his track for supplying intoxicating liquor to natives, this having been his practice for some time past.

It was three weeks before the messenger who had been

dispatched for the petrol returned with an ample supply. The airmen spent most of their time bathing in one of the lakes for which the celebrated oasis is justly famous – and there were no crocodiles – or resting in the shade of the palms. With their host they also visited the ancient ruins of the temple, and walked with awe over the stones that had been trodden by Alexander the Great and other men famous in history.

Kadar spent most of his time writing voluminous notes on his opinions and discoveries at the Lost Oasis, and these were in due course presented to an excited gathering of archaeologists in Alexandria, the city founded by Alexander the Great long before the birth of Christianity.

But at last, with its tanks filled, the Tourer stood at the end of a specially cleared runway, and they said goodbye to Kadar's father, who had decided to return by the more prosaic method which has been employed from time immemorial, that of a camel caravan.

One long day's flying saw the airmen back at Cairo, where they had a great reception and a civic ceremony, word of their discovery having preceded them. The jewels which they had found were, as Biggles had suspected, uncut gems of great value, and these were handed over to the authorities for disposal. Their sale realized a large sum, part of which was handed over to the explorers, and more than repaid them for the risks they had taken. Kadar, much to his delight, was also appointed an honorary curator of a well-known Egyptian museum where, as Biggles told him, he would be able to study antiquities to his heart's content without such attendant discomforts as thirst, scorpions, and crocodile sacrifices.

Sitting on the patio of the hotel where Kadar had first met them, Algy glanced suddenly at Biggles with a puzzled expression on his face but a twinkle in his eye.

'I seem to remember that when we first came here we were on our way to somewhere,' he murmured blandly.

'Quite right,' agreed Biggles. 'We were on our way to South Africa when Kadar came along with his bright idea for a joy-ride into the desert.'

'To a dinner of some sort, I think?'

'Quite correct,' agreed Biggles. 'If we started tomorrow morning we might still get there in time.'

Ginger yawned. 'Well, we seem to have seen all there is to see in Egypt, even things like oases which no one was quite sure existed. Sand is all right in small quantities, and it is even pleasant to look at by the seaside, but too much of it in one lump is apt to become monotonous. I, personally, am all for a change of scenery.'

'Yes, I feel that a nice green field or two would do our eyes no harm,' agreed Algy.

'Then if you'll be ready at the crack of dawn we'll tootle along southward,' Biggles told them, as he reached for the jug of iced lemon-squash that stood on the table.